JANJHAT

JANJHAT

ROOPLALL MONAR

PEEPAL TREE

First published in Great Britain in 1989
Reprinted in 2003
Peepal Tree Press Ltd
17 King's Avenue
Leeds LS6 1QS
England

ISBN 0 948833 30 0

This book is for Jeremy Poynting
whose efforts have made this novel possible

ONE

'Me neva dance-up so much since me could rememba, girl Sumintra,' Big-Bye mooma said. She was lying in a sugarsack hammock, slung between two house-posts under the bottom-house.

'Is true. But me feel like fire blazing in me body,' Sumintra replied, as usual chewing black tobacco. Three days after the wedding Big-Bye mooma and Sumintra felt drained. When they moved, their bones cracked like dry bamboo joints in the savannah sun, their eyes were sunken, their voices sounded like rusty zinc sheeting. When they coughed, lumps of cold phlegm lodged in their throats. Sumintra's eyes searched the yard; it looked like pig-pen. She spat out a mouthful of chewed tobacco.

Big-Bye mooma was reminded of a duck defecating as the clammy lump dropped on the grass. She felt a stab in her stomach as she looked at the well-kept grass bordering the bottom-house. She loved the grass. It reminded her of Manager Brown's front yard in the Plantation Compound, years back. She was one of the yard's gardeners. She had loved the grass and flowers...

Looking at her own grass she was sure the chewed tobacco would stunt its growth. Women who chewed black tobacco deserved a proper cut-rass from their husbands. But old Sumintra's husband was dead. Only an incurable sore-mouth could stop Sumintra from chewing black tobacco. Heh heh heh... if that should happen, at least her grass would be left in peace.

'An you t'ink me stoopid eh? Me choose am one good wife fo me Big-Bye,' she said with relish, smacking her tongue. She watched Big-Bye and his friends at the front of the house as they took down the bamboo and tarpaulin tents put up for the wedding.

Another group of older boys, shirts knotted, cigarettes stuck between their lips or on top of their ears, carried the benches out of the yard. They cackled like cocks ke ke ke over a wicked joke, but were careful to keep out of the women's hearing. They were afraid of Big-Bye mooma and Sumintra. Those two old women's tongues could lash deep, the curse-words gushing freely. Them women like real hatching fowl.

'Me believe so... Not everything shining like gold, is gold.' Sumintra did not sound so sure.

Big-Bye mooma, knowing Sumintra, winked in understanding. She settled in the hammock, sighing. This kiss-me-ass cold again. Is the white rum an' night dew. She coughed, trying to force a lump of cold phlegm out of her mouth. Her eyes watered. She coughed again and again. She felt exhausted. 'This blasted white rum,' she complained. 'They should stop make it. They say it have evil spirit inside.' She rubbed her chest and blinked her eyes. She felt her insides scorched. 'Shree Bhagawan, me neva feel so, if me could rememba good.' She added, 'Me know what you mean, Sumintra. But me still believe, by Shree Bhagawan grace, me choose one good wife fo me Big-Bye.'

Sumintra nodded. True, is everything look rosy and nice fo the first, but when the backlash come, it more bitter than senna. Heh heh... Sumintra pondered... an where sugar fall down, ants bound fo come.

Sumintra had wondered about Data the first time she saw her, dressed in her bridal gear. Her eyes, lined with mascara, seemed to know too much. Her lips, luscious and lipsticked, suggested many things. Something told Sumintra that conflict would brew someday between Big-Bye mooma and Data. It going explode like rainfall cloud. Chu chu chu... Teeth an tongue going clash... O Shree Bhagawan, better me pray. High house an radio killing ahwe self-respect. All this Sumintra kept to herself, chewing rapidly. She spat another mouthful of chewed tobacco on the grass. She wanted to retch, still tasting stale liquor in her mouth.

The midmorning sun crept into the bottom-house, casting long shadows. Big-Bye mooma fanned herself with her hands and loosened her long, grey hair. Sumintra shifted on the bench, trying to avoid the sun, heaving and sighing. The wind hardly blew. The street, running in front of the house, bustled with activity.

'Like ahwe get no rain fo just now, girl,' Sumintra said. She was thinking about the ricefields. Over two months now and not a drop of rain. Is how the rice going grow? Backdam wuk not enough to move you footstep. Is like '58 when the sun want kill you fo three months. Rice... sugar... cow... fish... chu chu chu... all stifle like grass in dry pasture. Shree Bhagawan. Ow don't make it happen again. Was a terrible time. Rainbow in sky but no rainfall. Was like a plague.

Big-Bye and his friends were working quickly now. They took the benches and tables back to the Hindu temple across the dam on the edge of the blackwater stream. Only the wares – enamel cups, plates, and spoons packed in wooden trays – lay haphazardly under the bottom-house. There was now hardly any sign that a wedding had taken place.

Big-Bye mooma and Sumintra, heaving their flattened chests in-out, in-out, as the now freshening Atlantic winds wafted under the bottom-house, were immersed in their own thoughts.

Is true. Me properly sport an dance. Me wonda how me foot coulda move so much, Big-Bye mooma remembered, echoes of the nagara drumbeats in her ears, mingled with jinglings from her silver anklets, thick and filigreed. Eh-eh, them nowadays young girls could properly move they behind. Bhanmattie and Lakeranie. Them girls could dance. They bubby been shaking like coconut in tree top. And they fat behind been swaying like snake as if they hip-bone is spring. She could not have danced with such abandon when she was a young wife, with the men ogling like hawks, their drunken eyes on your behind, everytime you swayed and swirled like bucktop. Never. Had she danced like that she would have been a dead woman a long time.

'Is what shame and disgrace you bring in this house,' her father-in-law or husband would have accused, shouting and whipping her with a varnished mango hackia.

'You want am drag ahwe good name in de gutter? Want am people spit on ahwe, eh? Is dis ahwe culture? Only blackman doam dat,' the father-in-law would have said, directing his son how to punish her.

Never. She shook her head as if waking up, blinking and trying to focus her eyes.

'What happen Big-Bye mooma?' Sumintra asked, concerned.

'Is nothing. Is just the wedding. Eh-eh, since backra gone, young gal foot come long like coconut tree. Ever notice the high heel and short dress? This Bhanmattie and Lakeranie is something eh. Wonda if they does pray? Get Gaad in they mind?'

'Girl, don't talk. Is more you live, is the more you see,' Sumintra said.

'Me wonda how Bhanmattie and Lakeranie husband them does feel when they moving they behind like spring?' Big-Bye mooma asked.

'Is only they husband know,' Sumintra chuckled. What was it people said? 'Is the more you could wine, the better the man like you in bed.' Is the Bombay film, and juke-box responsible for that, she reflected, wishing she, too, could dance like Bhanmattie and Lakeranie. Oh she would be the centre of attraction at wedding-houses, nine-day houses and engagements. But she would still continue her Sunday morning pujas and visiting the temple. Only thing is what she had for the men to look at? Just wrinkled skin, bony thighs and flattened hips. Never mind her thighs contained fire, especially when she had drunk white rum. It was different in cane-field days. Then she had cursed lustful drivers who had raped cowed women in the weeding gang. Which man would oblige her now? Eh-eh, an old, darkskin woman in her sixties, her breasts shrunken, her hair turning white, tobacco-smelling mouth. Who?

How could she have such thoughts at her age? Her duty was to perform household chores, spend more time doing devotion to Shree Bhagawan, visit the temple, act as god-mother to newly-born village babies, supervise funeral-houses. Because she was a widow, such tasks were given to her automatically. Everyone expected it; she was supposed to be wise, her experience vital to the village women.

But how to damp down the heat the white rum fired in her? She wished her husband were alive. It would have been his duty. After all me is still a woman. She spat out another lump of chewed black tobacco, her eyes roving between flowers and the redbrick street.

'Ow me Gaad!' Big-Bye mooma shouted suddenly, waving her hands.

Sumintra leapt off the bench as if she had seen a snake. Her heart pounded and in her surprise she swallowed what was left of the black tobacco in one gulp. She looked around, following Big-Bye mooma's eyes. 'What happen? What happen?' she asked in panic.

'O Gaad! Me good good oleander!' Big-Bye mooma cried. She leapt out the hammock, heading for the yard.

Sumintra followed, the black tobacco blazing in her stomach.

Big-Bye mooma stooped by a clump of oleander root, the stems broken, the leaves dry and crumpled. Big-Bye mooma clasped the root, tears streaming from her eyes.

'Is just here me does do me puja, Sumintra. Just here. Is what me going tell Shree Bhagawan?'

Sumintra felt awkward. She wanted to rush into the latrine in the backyard. This blasted black tobacco eat away half me inside. Is how me could drink white rum?

Big-Bye mooma implored, hands folded. 'Tell me, Sumintra?'

'Is them young boys dance on the oleander.' A group of boys had gathered at that very spot, drinking and dancing, ogling the girls who were dancing in the house and in the front verandah.

'O Gaad! Is what me going say?' Big-Bye mooma ran her fingers along the damaged stems. Then she arranged her clothes and got up. She dried her eyes with her skirt and stared at the oleander, then at Sumintra. 'If me catch that sonavabitch who mash up this oleander, me skin he like a duck.'

Sumintra flinched. Her bowels groaned.

'True Sumintra. Me rub he balls with vinegar an pepper. He playing man, eh. He destroy me oleander. When me done with he, he ain't good fo no woman. Gaad must direct me to him. Tru-tru. Me skin he like sheep. Tink cause he get balls he is a man.' Big-Bye mooma squared up, as though she wanted to fight.

Sumintra, though, was rushing for the latrine, Big-Bye mooma's words echoing in her ears.

By evening the fatigue of the day was beginning to wear off. Big-Bye mooma was calmer, though she still muttered about the sonavabitch who trampled the oleander. She had seen to it that all the utensils hired for the wedding were taken back to the Village Burial Society and after lunch she had cleaned the yard, sweeping and burning the dry, crumpled lotus leaves, provision pealings, food crumbs and fragments from broken bottles.

'Them people tink this is a pig-pen,' she grumbled, setting fire to the heap she had made in the street. As the embers flared the heap crackled. She felt better, wiping away sweat from her forehead. She wondered how she had managed to find the energy to clean the whole yard, feeling her muscles ache. But is Shree Bhagawan's work, she reasoned.

Then she had cooked the evening meal. Big-Bye and her husband, Loknauth, would relish the boiled split-peas, rice and curried shrimp. By late evening she had bathed and changed. Afterwards she lay in the hammock, waiting for Sumintra to visit.

'Me still feel miserable, Big-Bye mooma,' Sumintra said, entering the yard. She rubbed her chest, adding that she had visited the latrine three times after leaving Big-Bye mooma's yard. 'Girl, me believe me get griping. Talk 'bout belly-wuk. Eh-eh, one time me nearly mess-up the latrine seat. Good thing nobody was in the backyard. True, me behind exploding like bullet.' Sumintra sat gingerly on the bench.

Big-Bye mooma sniffed, her nose like a dog's searching a fowl pen, and blinked her eyes in disbelief. Gaad, dis woman. Good thing wasn't me latrine. Only this morning she'd had to clean hers, scrubbing the seat with a hard brush, a cloth wrapped over her nose. Still the smell lingered. She had retched twice, cursing those who used the latrine and messed the seat. 'Tink this is dungheap. Like they ain't get decency. Shitting like jackass...' When she held another religious work she would padlock her latrine. Let them use the street. Is food fo them dogs.

'Me whole inside blistering,' Sumintra said, still rubbing her chest and belching. Darkness crawled into the yard. A low wattage bulb cast a faint light under the bottom-house. Beetles groaned, crickets chirped and occasionally a firefly

13

flickered. There were lights in neighbouring houses and the sound of voices mingled with the clattering of pots and pans, a child's cry, a mother's reprimand. The street in front was deserted but for the dogs and a straying donkey.

'Still serious?' Sumintra asked, lowering her voice, flashing her eyes around. Big-Bye papa was out of sight.

'What you think, Sumintra? Take nothing fo granted. Don't make she looks fool you. Me done put aside the white cotton sheet. Tink me stoopid? Me no want no second hand wife in this house.'

'Is true,' Sumintra nodded. She smacked her lips and tasted bitterness in her saliva. A next visit to the latrine would kill her. O Gaad!

'You know what me and you pass thru,' Big-Bye mooma said...

Was thirty-six years ago; she had been married a week – at the age of fourteen when she knew nothing about sex and how babies were born. On the second Sunday night after the wedding, Loknauth, then a young boy of nineteen entered the darkened logie and lay down beside her, tight-lipped and nervous. He was shy. She was afraid, her heart pounding, body chilled. A few minutes later Loknauth turned to her and in a clumsy manner pulled out her panty. He struggled, panting. He parted her close-shut thighs. She didn't resist. It was her duty to remain passive. A burning sensation grew from inside her vagina as Loknauth penetrated, still acting as though caught in a wrestling match. He heaved and sighed, perspiration oozing from his body. She wanted to scream, to push him off. Something was trickling between her thighs; it felt thick and rancid. Then suddenly she felt warm juices inside her, mixed with the burning sensation. Loknauth slumped beside her, breathing heavily.

She had lain awake asking: Is this the sweetness young girls talk about? The sweetness that occurs when a man and a woman sleep together? It was after midnight when she slept.

14

In the morning, her mother-in-law, a chattering, small-built woman, accosted her in the logie. She held up a sheet, her eyes twinkling in satisfaction. 'Dis is de sheet you an me son sleep pon last night,' she said, pointing at uneven circles of dried blood. She had stared at the sheet, bewildered, ashamed.

'Me want to make sure you was a virgin. An dis is de proof. You is a propa Hindu picknee...'

So long ago, Big-Bye mooma said to herself. But the custom still prevailed. It was held to make the difference between a faithful or an unfaithful wife. But these present-day young girls: too much lipstick, high-heel shoe, short dress... eh-eh, going cinema, not doing regular puja. Now is hard to tell whether a Hindu girl is a virgin or not.

Sumintra couldn't fathom Big-Bye mooma's thoughts. But it was deep thinking.

'Hear the plan,' Big-Bye mooma whisperedat last, drawing close to Sumintra. Sumintra's eyes sparkled. 'Before Big-Bye and he wife going the bedroom fo sleep, me going done spread the sheet on the bed. When Big-Bye and Data in bedroom, you must go in to talk with Data to raise up she spirit. And make sure the sheet spread on the bed. You hear? You can't trust nowadays young gal. Me don't want to see more than what me seeing. Neva mind me choose am one good gal fo Big-Bye, me still want believe me own eye. Looks is not all! Is like trench water with no fish inside...'

Sumintra nodded, though she, herself, had never tested her daughter-in-law's virtue in this manner. She thought such an act was impudent, though sometimes she wondered if her second daughter-in-law had been a virgin when she married her son. She couldn't read her daughter-in-law. But she knew that her son loved her. Maybe he *had* taken her virginity. Beside, she seemed a good Hindu girl. She did her puja every Sunday morning, wore knee-length dresses.

'Everything fix, Sumintra,' Big-Bye mooma said, but

Sumintra had rushed out of the yard, heading for her latrine, farting and cursing the black tobacco.

Can't trust this time young gal. Me neva trust them more than me see them. They voice like honey and they body like gold. But more than one man done lay down on top them. Eh-eh, since this country get freedom is everything changing overnight. Them young gal daubing theyself with lipstick and powder and eye-lash pencil as if them in the circus. Eh-eh, soon time some gal going walk naked in the street... Yes, the short-short dress showing all they behind. Gaad, them gal na get shame. Is where the Hindu religion going? Big-Bye mooma wondered, scratching her grey hair, unaware that night was turning darker until Loknauth shouted from inside the kitchen. She sighed and heaved herself out of the hammock.

It was not long before they retired to bed. Loknauth's bones ached; he tired quickly these days. Big-Bye mooma lay awake.

'You can't trust thiefman this time,' she began. She wanted to make sure Loknauth had padlocked the fowl-pen, but he was snoring.

Big-Bye was still out with his friends, playing dominoes in Billy's Beer Garden in the back street. He wanted only that the second Sunday came faster. He couldn't contain his lust for Data.

TWO

The following Saturday Big-Bye felt an urgency mixed with sudden spurts of fear. At midday, lying on his bed, he tried to picture Data and how they would act in bed the next night. As he imagined her thighs, his penis hardened. He turned on his stomach, breathing hard, plagued by self-doubt. He wanted to operate with her as an experienced lover. His canecutting friends said, 'Hand the woman good in bed. After that you is she only man.' They were so confident when they discussed sex; they seemed to him so mature.

Unlike some of his friends who frequented the whore-houses in the city, he had never experienced sex, being afraid of catching the V.D. sickness he heard the older men talking about. He always found an excuse when his friends urged him to go with them on Saturday nights, but they never challenged his excuses and he was happy to let them think that he had his own scene of conquest, perhaps with somebody's wife. Had they known the truth, they would have laughed at him, so he kept his secret to himself.

Now he wished he had visited the whore-house, if only once. He cursed his stupidity. Just once and he wouldn't have caught anything. He wrestled with his plans. Gaad, me lolee like one piece of wood. His thoughts jostled like swimmers caught in an unexpected wave of memory.

He was about eleven years old. School was closed for the August holiday. Every midmorning during the weekdays he and his friends played a game called 'House'. Their parents had long since gone to work in the sugarcane fields two miles aback. It was a time when the sugar workers were still building their houses in the village, after moving out from the estate, though a few still lived in the Nigger Yard section, awaiting approval for their housing loans from the Sugar Labour Welfare Fund Committee. Most of the yards were still unfenced so it was easy for the children, boys and girls, to get together. For a time none of the elder brothers or sisters, who were also at home, took any notice of this game. They were just little children, out of harm's way, so Big-Bye and the others were left alone.

They usually played House in the fowl-pen. Before the game started Big-Bye would sweep out the pen, then spread sugarsacks on the wooden floor. If four girls were present, Big-Bye and his friends chose one girl each to act as their wives. As the game progressed they changed their partners.

At first, each pair would act as man and wife, aping their parents' mannerisms. Coconut shells and discarded odds and ends were used as cooking and household utensils in the game. About an hour later, before midday, each pair would claim tiredness, saying they would retire for the night. The girl-wife would lie down beside her boy-husband. Then the man and wife game would begin.

The images were blurred, but Big-Bye remembered pulling out the 'wife's' panty and the fumblings which both excited and made him feel he was doing something shameful and forbidden. He hadn't really known whether his lolee was meant to get inside the girl's patacake or not, and before long the 'husband' and 'wife' would feign sleep.

The House-game usually ended around one in the afternoon, the girls walking across to their respective homes, the boys heading for the cow-pasture to sling-shot birds and talk about the girls.

This game went on for a while. One Wednesday midmorning Big-Bye's friends didn't appear. It was a warm day, and the neighbourhood was quiet. Fowls cackled about and dogs hunted the fowl-pens. Only two girls showed up for the game. They helped Big-Bye clean the fowl-pen, then the game began. Both girls played Big-Bye's wives.

Suddenly a voice exploded like a balloon outside the fowl-pen: 'Is what you all doing in there? Wickedness?'

Big-Bye and the girls froze, hearts beating. They looked up, fright in their eyes.

'Open the door,' the voice demanded.

Big-Bye leapt off the girl, and hastily buttoned his crotch, fingers trembling. The girls pulled up their panties and got up, ashamed. The fowl-pen was locked from inside.

'Open the damn door before me break it down,' the voice demanded again, hands rattling the door. Big-Bye recognised the voice as one of the girls' elder sister. He imagined the blows he would receive that afternoon from his father. He opened the fowl-pen door and emerged feeling sick with fear. The girls followed. They were pupils now in front of the schoolmaster, obedient and repentant.

The girl's sister, a sixteen year-old sewing apprentice with fiery eyes and a lewd tongue, looked sharply at them, gesticulating with maternal sternness. She shouted, 'Take out you bloomers and raise up you frock,' pointing at the girls. The girls obeyed immediately, imagining the blows in store for them.

The girl's sister bent to examine them intently, one after the other. She shook her head.

Big-Bye wanted to run, to escape to the cow-pasture.

'Open you crotch,' the girl's sister turned to Big-Bye, her tone harsh and threatening. Big-Bye scrambled for the buttons and unloosed them. The girl bent down and examined him like a nurse.

'Good!' she exclaimed, rising and looking satisfied.

Big-Bye bolted, heading for the sea-wall. He was in agony the whole afternoon, suffering bouts of nervous trembling. He planned excuse after excuse to tell his parents. Truly he was ashamed. He counted the hours that would hasten the evening. But after three days nothing had happened. The girl's sister evidently hadn't told anybody.

News of the discovery spread to the other children and the game stopped for a week. Big-Bye avoided the girls. But his friends and other girls resumed the game more clandestinely in another fowl-pen. Sometimes Big-Bye could not keep away, but in truth he had lost the taste for the act.

As he grew older the shame of being caught in such a game grew stronger, though there were nights when the temptation to indulge in it gripped him strongly. But whenever he was tempted he would think of his parents.

'A proper Hindu boy don't do wickedness,' his mooma would say, as if she knew what was in his mind.

As Big-Bye wrestled with the pillow he ejaculated unexpectedly. He felt both release and annoyance at the spreading stain soiling his underwear.

'Shit. Meself gat to wash this.' His mooma could never be allowed to see this. Then he fell into fitful sleep.

When his mooma did appear at his bedroom door he was just waking up. 'Is after four now, Big-Bye,' she warned.

'Just now.' He was impatient and slightly agitated. This woman, he sighed. He got out of bed, opened the side window and examined his underwear. Shit. He had not yet worked out his approach to Data. He blinked a few times, inhaling draughts of freshly blown wind, trying to revive from his drowsiness.

'Is only when you hand the woman, the thing good in bed, then she respect you.' The words haunted him, echoed and re-echoed in his mind. If only he'd had sex just once he would have known what to do. He cupped his forehead and lamented, wondering if Data had any sexual experience. Young, unmarried girls were wise these days. The way they dressed could tell you. They frequented the cinemas, wore high-heel shoes and daubed their lips with lipstick. Some get boyfriends. Like this time young girl going mad, his mooma would say.

But he doubted whether Data had any sexual experience. She looked so shy. She had barely looked at him on the previous Sunday night after she had taken off her bridal-gear. When he attempted to talk to Data, she acted like a child, withdrawn, and fearful, seeking the chaperone's protection, though the old woman upbraided her with her eyes.

But what was it Bahadur had said? 'Never make a woman' look fool you. The more she nice, is the more she deep.' It had been a bright afternoon and the boys were playing cards by the street-end. Villagers and sugar workers passed to and fro. Big-Bye was watching the game. After a few hands, one of the boys, Lalo, asked Bahadur why he changed wives every two years.

'Aha boy,' Bahadur said humorously, lighting a cigarette, procured from on top of his left ear, 'All you youngster have a lot to learn.' He paused. 'Never learn to judge a woman by she looks. The more they beautiful, the more they sharp like razor. The moment they husband can't afford to dress them up, they turning outside. And where you think they end-up? Eh-eh, Under one next man belly. Sometime two man, three man...'

Bahadur looked slowly around him, inhaled the cigarette smoke, relishing it like food. He exhaled leisurely, exposing his tobaccostained teeth. His grin was mischievous. 'The moment one woman find you stoopid, they treat you like puppy. Check and see. Specially them nice woman who get ugly husband. Check again. All them smart women get stupid husband. Know why?' Bahadur stared beyond the boys' heads down the street leading to the sea-wall.

Big-Bye and the boys waited with rapt attention. They stared at Bahadur, agreeing among themselves, 'Bahadur proper study women.'

'Because women is pretensive animal,' Bahadur added. 'They could sweet-talk, then stab you behind you back.

21

They would lie down with another man, and doubt you in front you face. You hardly find a good Hindu woman today. Nice house full they eye. Is everybody come selfish after independence. No closeness anymore. Young gal want to live Town life. They losing they self-respect...'

Bahadur was right, the boys thought. He talked from experience. True. Bahadur was not a good-looking man. He was darkskin, short, and squatty with a broken tooth which stank. But he always had good-looking women as his wives.

'Bahadur is a real sweet man, you hear. And if he ain't get something to pull them women, skin me alive...' folks living in the village remarked whenever it was known that he had taken another wife.

Bahadur couldn't be wrong, Big-Bye told himself. There was no doubt he had a knack. Whenever he felt his wives were getting too smart, visiting the city too often, getting too great a taste for expensive clothes, he would turn suspicious. Acting smart like a cat baiting a rat, Bahadur always ended up catching his wives with other men. Whenever that happened the women's excuse would be that Bahadur was lazy, that he only liked to ride them every night as if they were mares.

'Lazy?' Bahadur would glare. 'Like them women want me kill meself in the canefield?' He earned his living catching fish in the blackwater canals in the backdam, two-three miles aback and selling them in the village. 'Is better to be independent so you could know you true purpose in life,' he said when people urged him to find a regular job.

Big-Bye felt more composed now. Yes. He knew how he would operate. Data could never out-manoeuvre him. Me is the man. He emerged out the bedroom and headed for the bathroom, a towel wrapped around his waist.

It took Big-Bye about ten minutes to bathe and change, sprinkling a bit of perfume on his clothes and carefully combing his hair. After a hasty dinner of boiled split-peas, rice, curried eddoes and calaboo, he was ready to go out.

'You better don't drink tonight. Remember tomorrow,' his mooma warned him in the kitchen downstairs. His papa was working in the back garden, tending the pepper and bora plants. Later he would feed the fowls and lock them in the pen.

'And try and behave youself tomorrow,' his mooma added. All day she'd been chattering like a parrot. She, too, was waiting for the second Sunday night. She had to make sure Big-Bye didn't get a second-hand wife, to prove that her judgement of Data was right. You couldn't take anything for granted.

'All that glitters is not gold.' She couldn't get these words out of her head. Sunday night and Monday morning would decide whether Data was fit to live in this house.

When Big-Bye left the house, he headed straight for Bahadur's home in the Second Street. Bahadur's company might help increase his confidence for the following night. At least, Bahadur's jokes would ease his depression. But he wished he had experience of sex itself.

The village – only ten years before a burial ground and ricelands – was lively that evening. There were peddlers and hucksters at every street-head displaying their eatables. Children sauntered about while youths and married men thronged the rumshops, drinking and gaffing. Big-Bye was oblivious to all this. He thought only of Data and Bahadur.

'Ow Big-Bye, ow! You ain't hear what happen?' Bahadur's wife Suruj, his third, greeted Big-Bye as soon as he entered their bottom-house.

Suruj was a stout-built woman in her early thirties, a divorcee whom Bahadur had lured away from Mahaica, further up the East Coast, a year before.

Big-Bye was taken aback, startled. 'What happen?' he asked, as he sat on a rickety wooden bench.

'Ow me Gaad, Bahadur in the pelice station since this morning,' Suruj lamented, beating her chest dab dab.

'Station?' Big-Bye muttered, baffled. His hopes fell. Bahadur!

'Yes. Shakoor claim Bahadur and One-Foot tief he fowl and fowl-egg last night. You believe that?' Suruj rushed at Big-Bye, holding out her palms in a gesture of supplication. Raising her voice to attract the neighbours, she told him she believed one of them was responsible for Bahadur's predicament.

Big-Bye was speechless. 'Fowl?' he finally managed.

'Is only bad-minded people could think so. Shakoor tell the pelice One-Foot was outside, and Bahadur went in the pen. He say when he shout, One-Foot scramble out the yard like hop-an-drop, and so come One-Foot lef he crutch. Me believe One-Foot *was* there cause I know he is a fowl-thief. But I can't believe Bahadur was in the pen.' Suruj's face was clouded in sorrow. Then her eyes became ferocious, darting at the neighbouring houses, most of which were suspiciously quiet.

'If me catch Shakoor in dis yard, me skin he balls and fry it like sheep one,' she added passionately. 'And he got the pounce to tell the pelice he catch Bahadur red-handed in the fowl-pen, and feather was in Bahadur mouth. You could believe that? Bahadur is wicked, but he is not fowl-thief...'

Big-Bye suspected that Shakoor had set out to trap Bahadur. He knew Bahadur and Shakoor often threw remarks at each other, beginning from the time Suruj had come to live there. Shakoor claimed to know her from Blairmont Village when she was a teenager. He would say: 'Suruj not showing any respect fo the neighbourhood. Soon time she going eat pork and throw the bone in me yard.' He was an orthodox muslim, known for his piquishness. He attended the mosque across the Public Road every evening and unfailingly made his ritual daily ablutions. For this he was respected in the village.

'You wait til the pelice bail Bahadur. You wait. Me meself

would deal with this Shakoor. Tink me ain't know he tickling them bib-bib girls who does go to him to get they planet read. Tink me ain't know?' Suruj waved her hands offensively, pointing at Shakoor's house, which was opposite theirs. 'And if he is a man, let him come out,' she added, hoping Shakoor was hearing.

Big-Bye could not decide what the truth was. He felt that Bahadur was not a fowl-thief, but wondered how Shakoor had managed to trap him. He tried to console Suruj as best he could, before leaving, feeling depressed, though not without some pleasant imaginings of Suruj's breasts and her naked body.

THREE

The first time Data menstruated she panicked. She thought she had suffered a cut between her thighs. She was thirteen years old and had been taken out of school two months before, when her mother noticed her breasts had begun developing.

It was a Friday, around eleven o'clock in the morning. She had just finished the housework. Feeling tired and sweaty, she decided to take a bath. She changed into an old dress and tattered underwear, and headed for the blackwater stream which ran in front of the house, winding its way towards Plantation Lusignan. It was a drab day of faint sunlight, the clouds heavy-set, birds twittering sleepily in the trees aback the houses. The redbrick road running in front of the houses was deserted but for the occasional iron-wheeled dray cart which rumbled to and fro, loaded with grass and shopkeepers' groceries. Data waited for one to pass, driven by an especially unkempt man who leered at her, spitting out a stream of black tobacco and lashing his beast violently. Data felt all too conscious that her parents were working in the sugarcane fields several miles away.

At last he had passed. Data stood on the wooden ghat, at the edge of the stream near the wooden bridge that led into their yard. She looked around. It was quiet. At least no boys were around. She knew they liked nothing better than to loiter whenever a grown-up girl was bathing in the stream. The boys were wicked. They teased the girls, making lewd signs with their fingers, pointing at the girls' bottoms. At least I'm safe, Data told herself.

She stepped down from the wooden ghat, and slowly, carefully, waded in the stream, shivering slightly in the cold, dark water. She bent down, the water submerging her body, only her neck exposed. She rubbed herself vigorously, shivering and sighing. She flapped her feet and hands, trying to swim. Water real cool, she told herself, floating now, and sputtering mouthfuls of water.

She wanted to learn to swim; it was a good exercise and you feeling nice, but: 'Swimming is not proper for young girl,' her mother always warned, her voice tinged with some nameless fear.

Mummy must be know something. Jumbie! Eh-eh, them old people say evil spirit live in the water. But so long me never see one. Then suddenly her eyes widened with fear. She remembered hearing the stories of water-mama. Half-fish, half-woman. They lived under the water. If they liked you, they would bait you until you were tempted to swim in that part of the water where water-mama usually roamed. Then with a sudden plash, like a big fish breaking the surface, they would paw you and pull you down to their underwater kingdom. You would never return. To friends and family you were dead. Data knew of many tales about missing children who had last been seen playing by lonely streams, victims, according to the tellers, of water-mama. She shuddered.

But nothing happened, and as Data waded cautiously in the water, her thoughts strayed to more common threats – the boys who liked to peep at girls. Them feel they is big-man. Them girls say they like show out them thing. Shake it at you. Is wonder why?

Data floated, kicked her feet like a duck, her dress rising, hair loose. Aah, she sighed, feeling her muscles relaxing. She looked around. No eyes were on her. She floated in abandon, flexing her feet as if riding a bicycle.

Suddenly she stopped as if paralysed. She felt a griping pain in her belly and the feeling that something was oozing out of her inside, then a tingling sensation as if crawling worms moved inside her. 'Swimming is not proper fo young girl,' her mother had said countless times to her and her sisters. In panic, she waded out of the stream, heading for her bedroom. She took off her wet clothes. Her cotton pants were seeped with blood and stuck to her thighs. She took them off, puzzled. She examined herself, looking for the cut. No cut could be seen, but warm blood, darkish in colour, oozed slowly like sap from a gum tree from between her legs. This is what? she asked herself.

God, if mummy know, what she would say? She cleaned herself up and vowed not to bathe in the stream again. Is the stream cause the bleeding. An evil spirit. From now on me have to be careful when me wash clothes and dishes on the ghat. Next time water-mama go take me under the water. As she lay in bed, waiting for her two smaller sisters to arrive home from school for the midday meal, she continued to wonder why the blood. Was it water-mama's doing? Her heart fluttered, belly ached.

She felt suffocated in the big bedroom though wind wafted through the thatched roof. It was a clean-looking house made of wood, resting on three-foot stilts; it had been built by her grandfather, an old India-born man who had come as a bound labourer to Plantation Lusignan when he was sixteen. He had never gone back to India, but settled near the estate, working as a free labourer. When he had died the house had become her father's. Data turned restlessly, still wondering.

By evening the pain was unbearable. She had changed two panties, both soiled with blood. She had to tell someone but not her mother. Oh no, her mother would fret like a hatching fowl, waving her hands. She would ask what madness sent Data to bathe in the stream. 'You is a man?'

O God, that was too much. Better tell someone else, Data reasoned, wondering who.

Two evenings later.

'Stoopid, me chile,' old Sushila muttered, waddling in her half-lit logie. 'You tun woman now, chile. You could make picknee, heh heh heh...' Sushila laughed, exposing her toothless gums.

Data looked baffled. She thought Sushila, whom she trusted, was making a joke of the matter, this same Sushila who healed women's belly pain, helped the midwife deliver babies for village women. Could she be serious? Data felt confused as she sat on a low wooden bench.

'You na understand, me chile? Mean that you could married and bear picknee.' Sushila chuckled. She was a hefty, light-skin woman, whose silver anklets and bracelets jingled as she moved. Her voice was husky and deep. It thundered when she was angry. Little children were afraid of her when they met her on the road, bulldozing her way into the grocery, eyes penetrating, tapping her walking stick.

'Married! How?' Data wanted to know, her eyes pleading.

'Every woman have to bleed one time in the month, me chile, else them is no good woman.' Sushila sat beside Data, sighing as if tired, and began explaining the intricacies of the menstrual cycle, and the mysteries of childbirth.

Data took it all in, her eyes fascinated like a traveller in another world. She began to understand. Knew why boys showed girls their thing... why boys wanted to peep between girls' thighs and see their patacake.

Sushila turned serious, fixing her gaze on her husband's picture hanging on the crusted wall. Data followed Sushila's eyes. She remembered a story she had heard about Sushila and her husband...

It was said that he had stolen one of Sushila's silver pendants, pawned it and spent two days drinking away the proceeds. When Sushila discovered the theft, she was furious.

She had caught him in the rumshop, clutched him by the seat of his pants and dangled him gasping above the table. Then, so the story went, he had messed his pants in fear before being dumped on the ground by his cursing wife.

Another story Data had not been supposed to hear concerned the night the village had found Sushila on top of her husband, pinning him struggling and screaming to the earthen floor. He was naked from the waist down and she was threatening to wring-out his balls because he had been friendly with another woman. People said Sushila had driven her husband to drink himself to death.

'And don't go about flaunting you behind all about the place like them other girl,' Sushila cautioned.'This time young girl tink they see the sun before me. Can't wait til they get married. Eh-eh, they pussy scratching them. And when they finish doing they wickedness, they come to Sushila. "Ow, granny Sushila, ow, me no see me monthly. Help me." And when me examine them, is what you think chile? Eh-eh, the more you live, the more you see... Is man thing-a-ling been go inside. This time young girl hot like fire. Me tell you... No self-respect at all.'

Sushila headed for a side window, hawked and spat. 'Yes, you know how much young gal secret Sushila know? Anytime you feel you pussy run hot, bathe it out. You hear me? Never make one cocky go in it til you get married.'

Data walked home slowly after she left Sushila's house, past the kerosene lamps flickering in houses nestling on each side of the road, past the crickets and beetles noising among the bushes. She was silent and withdrawn for the rest of the evening.

From then on Data knew she had to safeguard her virtue, that she had to be careful and restrained. At the same time she became more interested in her appearance, always looking at herself in the bedroom mirror. And more and more frequently, especially in the evenings, she was immersed in her own thoughts.

Data was too embarrassed to tell her mother that she had started menstruating, but she suspected her mother knew. Whenever her periods came, the accompanying symptoms – belly-pain, back-ache, dizziness and an irritated temper – were obvious. Her mother would be gentle and affectionate during these times, telling Data to rest. She would delegate the house-chores to the sisters, and make indirect remarks about the reason.

As weeks passed into months her mother noted that Data was blooming into a desirable young woman. She more lovelier than me was at she age, she thought, watching Data playing hopscotch with neighbouring girls on the road. At least, she body more shapelier an' she skin lighter and she don't have to work in the canefields. She'd worked from the age of twelve, collecting and burning canetrash with girls her own age. She'd earned two shillings a week, good money in those days, which helped run the house.

Was such a long time... She had lived with her parents in a one-bedroom logie in the Nigger Yard section of Plantation Lusignan. The logie had an earthen floor, and leaked whenever rain fell, bringing out the cockroaches and wood-ants from the walls and rooftops. At fifteen she had married Data's father and they had lived in another logie on the same estate. Seven years later they had come to live in this house, about two hundred rods away from the Nigger Yard. It was Data's grandfather's house.

One night, about a year after Data had begun menstruating, her mother accosted her father. Data and her two sisters were in the smaller bedroom, telling stories. Rain drizzled outside.

'You know what, man? Time enough fo send Data to sewing,' her mother said, lying on the bed beside her husband.

'After one year or two we going chose a good boy fo she,' she added, seeing herself a bride's mother, garbed in the traditional yellow sari, jewels jingling on her body.

31

Data's father, a cautious man weathered by hard work, coughed twice and put out his cigarette. 'Is true woman,' he said quietly, hands resting on her hips. 'Mean we have to save money. When wedding come we got to have enough.'

'When time come we going manage,' Data's mother replied; the two cows they owned and the acre of riceland they rented from the Plantation would help to bring in the extra money.

'Anyhow, you must keep one eye on she,' Data's father said in a gruff tone, turning on his other side. 'You can't trust them young boys this time. They feel they getting too big. If I ever catch one of them whistle-whistle at Data me going cut out he balls, or bury he head in the trench. No Gaad in they mind.'

Data's father remembered his own father's words, spoken in Hindi, of course: 'Self respect is the greatest virtue in this world, son.' Shame and disgrace must never fall at me door. Oh no! People would say me is just a dungheap who pretend to be respectable. A nincompoop. They would spit insultingly whenever they see me walking the redbrick road.

Data's mother knew her husband meant everything he said. She vowed to take extra care of Data's movements, to keep a sharp eye on the boys whenever they loitered around her. No belly in me house before marriage, she told herself, trying to sleep.

'Girl, you betta careful. Me hear something,' Anjanie exclaimed, jerking her fingers to and fro, her eyes in panic.

'What happen?' Data asked anxiously.

It was a mid-week morning. Data's parents had gone to work, and the two younger sisters had left for school. Data was about to set off for her sewing class in a house on the other side of the village. Anjanie usually accompanied her .

'Girl, is where you does throw way you monthly cloth?' Anjanie asked, staring at Data.

'Is why you asking, girl?' Data questioned, unsettled.

'Girl Data, the pandit say Charandai get sick cause Charandai does throw way she monthly cloth all about the place. The pandit say evil spirit catch Charandai monthly cloth, and go straight in she patacake.'

Data was taken by surprise. 'Evil spirit? Jumbie!'

'Is true, girl. Charandai talking madness, and she bleeding. And she leg and patacake scale-up like she get leper.'

'Since when it happen?' Data asked. At least she, herself, was safe from this evil spirit. Her mother had cautioned her, in her usual roundabout way, that young girls should throw away their monthly cloth in the latrine pit. Data made sure she always did that. Data tried to imagine Charandai's condition. Poor child. They were of the same age. But Charandai was fatter, and her interests ranged between Bombay films and boys.

'But why Charandai?' Data asked. Must be man-jumbie... Data knew that sometimes village girls claimed that sometimes men-jumbie would sleep with them in the night, caressing them and making love to them. Data suspected this had some connection with their menstrual cloth. A few of these girls became pregnant. Others recruited Sushila's help. Parents of such girls were looked upon by village folks as outcasts.

'God, if that ever happen to me, me father kill me,' Data shuddered.

'From now on me go make sure me throw away me monthly in the latrine. Me na want no jumbie catch me,' Anjanie promised, her eyes fearful. 'Dem ole people say that when evil spirit hold you monthly one time, it coming back on you steady-steady. You losing all you picknee when you get married. And you always bleeding.' She got up and paced the floor, adjusted her dress, before bolting out of the house saying: 'Me hustling home befo rain come down. Betta careful with you monthly cloth.'

Data watched Anjanie scurry away. Anjanie and Charandai! Data smacked her tongue. Those girls loved to wallow in village rumours, 'This woman friendly with that man... Big-Head going round with Prandai... Gobin wife does meet Sewa by the mango tree anytime Gobin dead drunk...' They would pick up and exaggerate such stories with relish. True. Every-time a villager discovered an unmarried boy and girl doing wickedness aback someone's house, or holding hands clandestinely, Anjanie and Charandai would make such discovery a big issue. News spread fast in the village.

'They ain't get shame!' Anjanie would say, hawking and spitting as though she scorned the culprits involved.

'Them deserve one proper cut-rass,' Charandai would say, laughing heh heh heh, swaying her hip like a duck's behind.

Data tried to ignore such gossip and the scandalous remarks at funeral houses and religious ceremonies. She was a good Hindu. To indulge in such trifles would bring untold punishment to herself and her parents. 'Shree Bhagawan seeing everything,' her mother often remarked.

Data was especially uncomfortable when Anjanie and Charandai indulged in what she thought were wicked pranks, such as parading around with only panties on in Data's home, in the absence of her parents and sisters. To berate them was to risk being labelled a prude, so Data would adopt an attitude of detachment, as if enveloped in faraway thoughts.

One day Anjanie and Charandai had gone further. The three were alone. Anjanie had pulled down her panties.

'This is ting,' she had boasted. It was too much for Data. She had gone to the window and looked out nervously in case anyone should come. She would have nothing to do with this rudeness, and though they invited her to join in the exhibition, she ignored them, sitting glum and with-drawn, only occasionally glancing at her friends, feeling relieved when they left her house.

As Data bloomed, her hips broadened, her firm breasts became more noticeable. She began to act like a grown-up woman, helping her mother to manage the household, watching over her two small sisters and sometimes telling them off when they vexed her. She went with her mother to the Sunday morning pujas and other temple functions, and to the kathas and other ceremonies held in peoples' homes. After a time the boys began calling Data 'Chuch woman.' And whenever her parents exploded in quarrels, Data pacified them. She felt it was her duty.

'The more you live one straight life, the more people respect you,' Data heard her mother say when the neighbouring women gathered to talk during the evenings. The women sat on open sugar-sacks spread on the ground, in front of the house, little children prancing inbetween them.

'The moment you husband na find you good, he left you. You know how much shame and disgrace going come in you house? Eh-eh, is betta to drink one dose poison.'

Data had heard her mother use these words many times. She had said them when she heard the rumour that Sugrim's daughter 'got chase out' from her in-laws' home just two weeks after her marriage. It was said that the husband, a young canecutter, complained to his mother the next morning after the second Sunday, 'She na bleed.'

The other time concerned Chaitoo. It was said he had caught his second daughter doing wickedness with Rukmin's son aback his house, early in the night. Marriage took place only after Chaitoo had threatened the boy with a cutlass and told him: 'Me going to head-off you neck. Want throw me name in the drain?'

Data, on the other hand, was regarded by the village folks – apart from the youngsters who called her 'chuch woman' – as a straight and decent girl. The older people especially would greet her in a most friendly way whenever she was spotted walking on the road, or patronising one of the roadside sellers.

With the boys who leered and whistled at her she was stiff and withdrawn. Anjanie, on the other hand, always responded. 'Ayuh must seek-aff ahyuh sissy and mooma,' she barked, hawking and spitting as she quickened her footsteps up the road. The boys would laugh heh heh heh... 'Look how she wineing.'

But if Data avoided such ruderies, she could not help feeling that another world of experience lay somewhere beyond her. She had been intrigued one sunny afternoon when, sitting on the bench at the front the house, her eyes had run to Clara, a middle-aged married woman, and Sattie, a young unmarried girl, who were passing by, deep in conversation. Clara had blurted out words which echoed in Data's ears: 'Is true girl. The more you could do the thing in bed, the betta the man like you.'

The mystery of those words remained with Data for weeks. At times she was tempted to ask Anjanie or old Sushila, but prudence restrained her. Doggedly she dissected the words, each one, until she believed she under-stood their meaning. But in spite of her curiosity about sex, the mystery of menstruation and developing breasts, not once did Data try to investigate or seek pleasure in her body. She knew of other girls who did such 'commonness', those acts which were a betrayal of the purity of a good Hindu girl.

When Data was seventeen, her mother announced quite casually: 'We get one boy fo you, Data. Is time enough you get married.' It was a Sunday morning. She and her mother had come back from the temple after doing puja. Yes, Ma. She didn't insist that she was too young. Yes, Ma. She didn't question her mother about the boy. Yes, Ma. She didn't rage or even fume inwardly.

No. It was her duty to get married. To produce children. It was only after you had done that you fulfilled part of your womanhood. That she knew.

'And the boy cutting cane in the backdam. He look quiet,' the mother said a week later.

'What is decreed in the stars cannot be avoided,' the pundit would say at the end of the temple ceremonies.

Data understood. But there was no anticipation, no counting of the days until the marriage took place. And she admitted to herself that she would have liked to marry a teacher, or a civil servant.

FOUR

'You better make sure the sheet on the bed, Sumintra. You can't take chance with this time young gal. Though me mind tell me, me make one good choice, still looks could deceive you,' Big-Bye mooma cautioned. She had already taken two shots of white rum, though she had promised herself not to drink after last week's session.

Sumintra stood alongside, their conversation quiet. 'Can't trust people nowadays. They get donkey ears. They like hear other people story, not they own,' Big-Bye mooma added, glancing around at the neighbouring houses, looking to see whose prying eyes might be there. When she was certain nobody could overhear them, she continued talking with Sumintra.

It was the second Sunday, one week after the wedding. Big-Bye had already left the house, though not before he had listened to several lectures from his mooma on what clothes he should wear and how he should mind his manners. He was even more excited and anxious than he had been all week when he set out to collect Data from her village, Lusignan, a mile away to the west, half a mile inland from the Public Road.

There was a flurry of excited activity when the hired maroon Vauxhall pulled up in front of Data's house. Data's two sisters, fluttering like birds, rushed outside to welcome Big-Bye. Data's father came out looking happy and proud and escorted Big-Bye into the house. Her mother, hovering in the background, smiled shyly.

Big-Bye was invited to sit on a wooden chair by a round, varnished table. He felt unsettled, sweat oozing from his armpits. Data's mother placed a small bowl of curried chicken on the table. 'Eat son,' she urged, sighing happily.

Big-Bye nibbled at the chicken and hardly touched the white rum. Mind your manners, boy, echoed his mooma's words. He spoke quietly and only when spoken to. He had to give the impression that he was a quiet, decent young man, but his eyes darted at Data every time she padded through the house, apparently ignoring his presence.

Other women, whom Big-Bye suspected were Data's neighbours, scurried about the house, glancing at him, smiling, anticipating the sporting that would follow after Big-Bye and Data left. Occasions such as these gave them a chance to unshackle their pent-up feelings. Each shot of white rum drew them closer to each other. Then they would begin dancing and singing.

This was their custom, to sport after the bride and bridegroom had left, the singing and the dancing ending only when the men turned boisterously loquacious, their talk exploding in nostalgic memories. Then the scent of bhoonjal chicken, boiled split-peas, mango achaar and rice would fill the house. This had been the work of the women cooking in the low, wooden, thatched-roof kitchen aback the house, sneezing with the smoke, savouring the food with spoons, smacking their tongues.

'When you take wife, you tun big man, son, you have to tink ten year ahead,' Data's father advised, drinking the white rum freely, and sighing in commiseration. His bloodshot eyes were deep-set, his stubbled face a mixture of seriousness and geniality. Big-Bye didn't look straight at him; that was deemed disrespect – a first son-in-law to look his father-in-law in his face. Never happened. But Big-Bye liked the man.

'And don' matta how backdam wuk like rockstone, eh-eh, you is man enough to conquer. Tink of ahwe ole people. If they na had faith, tink they woulda survive?' Data's father added.

Big-Bye nodded dutifully, his eyes wavering everytime Data, or one of her sisters moved about in the house. The sisters marched around in a sprightly, knowing way; they, too, were sewing apprentices; they imagined themselves as brides, envying Data in an affectionate, sisterly way.

'When you married, is fo life time,' echoed Data's mother, a short, squattily built woman.

She stood near her husband, fanning herself and complaining about the heat, her dream fulfilled, the dream of every mother to see her eldest daughter married. 'And a decent marriage, too, beside,' she had chuckled a few days ago to some of her friends at Sewnath's katha. 'And the entire village attend Data wedding, gal. And they eat two-three time you know...'

'Once you and you wife live good, nobody could point they finger and say you eye black. Never.' Her face hardened as she said this to Big-Bye. 'This time generation quick to give you bad name. Them young gal fuget they culture and self-respect. Is too much cinema and radio and lipstick. Eh-eh, long time was different... Think me could watch me modin-in-law in she face? Is long dress and ornhi you wearing when you going out. And is no back ansa. Is yes ma, and no ma. Never mind living been hard but ahwe ole people use to live like one family.' She got up and headed for the bedroom.

'Is true,' Big-Bye nodded, but his interest was elsewhere. He was curious to know what was going on in the big bedroom. Data, her sisters and two youngish married women were inside, their voices crackling in jokes. Big-Bye knew Data was being dressed, but why should two women be with her? Like Data ain't know how to dress? He always admired girls who dressed fancy – pants, short dresses, lipstick, powder – but his mooma... Oh, she was against that. 'Not propa fo Hindu gal dress so. That fo black gal,' she would snap whenever she spotted a Hindu girl in a short dress.

An hour later Big-Bye was feeling restless. Data's father, now drunk, had lapsed into a confused monologue of sorrow and suffering. 'If only me as boy coulda read and write, tink me woulda be in canefield licking the backra man behind. Heh heh heh... me woulda be book-keeper like Khan. If only me coulda read... but when you tink of it, is ahwe own sardar, ahwe driva make it hard. True. When you you tink bout it, the white people not so bad after all...'

Data's father moved without warning between self-accusation, bitter heckling at his fate and resigned laughter, beating his hairy chest as if gripped by an insidious chest cold. He coughed repeatedly, struggling for breath, his eyes watering. 'Is, is the rain an sun. Tink it easy to cut cane in rainfall when sun catch you in the field?' He struggled with the words. 'If only me coulda read an write, me coulda wuk in the office...'

After regaining his composure, though his eyes still watered, he urged Big-Bye to drink, patting him affectionately, calling him son. Big-Bye refused politely, smiling: 'You drink, Pa.' Data's father obliged, then he lapsed into another monologue, breaking occasionally into song – a mixture of Hindi melodies and creole rhymes – punctuated by coughs and curses. 'Fowlcock a knack drum; Guinea bird a dance. O ho ho ho...'

In the kitchen, Data's mother and a group of older women, were talking in muffled voices, testing and commenting on the dishes being cooked.

Big-Bye got up and stretched, eyes still darting at every female who flurried between the bedroom and the kitchen. He felt uncomfortable now, gazing through the side window towards the ricefields and canefields further down. He knew those places, recalling when he and friends went searching the fields, looking for cowdung, shooting at birds, catching fish. He'd been about fourteen then. He felt a stiffness in his muscles, then an urge to urinate. The damn time going so slow. Data taking so long to dress. He heard

41

the giggling, and joking coming from the big bedroom and wondered. He leant on the window-beam to hide his discomfort, his perfumed, shaven face tightening as he tried to stifle the irritation he felt in his bladder. Shit, if me ask fo the latrine, is what them people going to say? He recalled his mooma's advice: 'Mind you manners, son.'

In agony Big-Bye turned, strode up and down, then sat on the couch. Feigning tiredness, he closed his eyes as he reclined, trying to take his mind off his discomfort by imagining how Data would look...

A few minutes later he became aware that two men had entered the house and were helping themselves to the rum. At first they grumbled gruffly. Then they downed their shots in one gulp, smacked their tongues, and tried to awaken Data's father. Big-Bye still reclined, though with his eyes open now. The two men playfully taunted the women in the kitchen. They sniffed the air, exclaiming, 'Aha! Chicken curry.' They clicked their tongues as if beating a drum, and stomped their feet softly.

'Gaad. Ahwe going to sport today like rig-jig,' the thin-built, meagre-faced one blurted out, smacking his lips.

'Look like no wuk fo me tomorrow,' the other agreed. 'Is good thing me drink salt, an chase out de worms in me bowel. Me could eat an drink to belly-ful. An to hell wid de backdam wuk. Eh-eh, me been wukkin fo twenty years, an is what me gat to show? Not one damn thing.'

More jokes and laughter exploded from the kitchen. Every other minute Data's mother moved between there and the bedroom, fanning herself and fretting happily.

Finally Data walked out of the bedroom, followed by her sisters, excitement and happiness lighting up their faces. Data looked quite attractive, Big-Bye thought. He got up.

'Nice girl,' exclaimed one woman, envy furrowing her brow.

As Big-Bye and Data sat down to eat at the round table, now loaded with food, they were given gifts of money by the women. Those who didn't give money, offered gold jewellery. Data's mother gave her a gold chain and a pair of gold bangles. The women giggled. Afterwards Data kissed the women and her sisters, eyes stained with tears.

There was another flutter of activity as Big-Bye and Data walked out of the house and into the yard, though inside the house the men paid only the slightest attention to the departure. They were long settled to drinking and grumbling about their fate. Outside though, the women were gathered, hushed in sisterly feeling, recalling their days as brides.

Data's mother and her sisters shed tears as Big-Bye and Data were escorted to the back seat of the car. Another woman put Data's grip in the trunk. The chauffeur was tapping the wheel, impatient to go, thinking about the sport to come at Big-Bye's house.

'Keep good, me beti,' Data's mother mumbled between sobs. 'Care youself,' the sisters advised, standing near the car.

Data cried, wracked by a sudden emptiness. 'You gat to married one day,' she recalled her mother's words. She adjusted herself in the seat, careful not to touch Big-Bye. She tried to muffle her tears.

Big-Bye was ill-at-ease. Data's presence unsettled him. He inched towards the left window, watching the women clustered around the car. It was hot and airless inside.

'De dulaha want go home,' an old, toothless woman remarked. Laughter exploded. Data's mother wiped her tears with her orhni, bidding Big-Bye and Data goodbye. Neighbouring girls stood on the bridges in front of their houses, watching, wide-eyed.

The car sped out. Data's eyes were lowered. Big-Bye stared at the huts and unpainted houses thronging both sides of the redbrick road, then at the Public Road when the car swung into it. He could not look at Data, but her presence was overwhelming his senses, her perfume tingling in his nose.

When they arrived at his house, his mooma was standing at the front gate to welcome them. She wore a saffron-coloured sari and her traditional silver jewellery. An ornhi was tucked across her grey head. She faltered slightly.

Big-Bye and Data, fingers clutched into each other's, stood dutifully on the wooden bridge. Data lowered her eyes bashfully. Big-Bye smiled, winking at the cluster of women and children standing in the yard, inspecting Data.

Big-Bye mooma spoke some words of welcome in Hindi, blessing Data as she passed a decorated, rice-pasted lota over their heads seven times. Afterwards she emptied the water from the lota in front of Big-Bye and Data, and beckoned them to enter the yard, and then the house. 'That clear all badluck,' she whispered.

Laughter and handclaps erupted as the tension broke. About a dozen of the women and children followed the couple into the house. Big-Bye mooma and Sumintra chatted all the way, their wrinkled faces bright, noses assaulted by the aroma of the mutton curry being cooked downstairs.

After being introduced to the neighbouring women and far-off relatives, Data was led by Sumintra into Big-Bye's bedroom. 'Lef doolahin in peace,' the old woman said.

Some of the women and young girls remained in the house, anticipating Data's return. They wanted to be the first to make her acquaintance. Outside, in the yard, some of the other women passed judgement:

'But she ain't so nice as when she been in doolahin clothes.'

'An' you know she bubby look flat. Eh-eh, wonder if she ever do the thing before?'

'Me na care what you all say, but she look like she get good ways...'

Under the house men and women were cooking and drinking. Two women sat in a corner, each beating a dholak while an old man, already drunk, sang biraha. As the drum-beats accelerated in unison with the singer's pitch, a rapid claphand followed. A few of the older women interrupted their chores and threw in a dance, encouraged by cackling mouths and cries of: 'Leh e go, leh e go!' More handclaps followed, tongues clucking with the drum-beats.

Big-Bye mooma felt good as she fretted happily, supervising the cooking and drinking. Occasionally she fired a look at Loknauth, whom she had warned not to drink too much, and whom she had made responsible for putting the correct amount of salt in the mutton curry.

'People quick to find fault nowadays,' she had told him earlier that morning. 'And is a shame if people say food na taste good. Is betta you daub black-pot on you face. How it going look? You invite people and you can't feed them properly.'

'Is true,' Big-Bye papa had said, leaving to join the men in the backyard. They were skinning the sheep, the carcass hanging on a mango tree. Though it was early in the morning the men sweated, chattering about the many sheep they had slaughtered in the past for occasions such as these. They delighted in their task, contemplating a tasty curry. Occasionally they took a snap from a bottle of brown rum, smacking their tongues aha. They treated the carcass with respect, as though enacting a ritual.

'Nothing beat de estate days, eh!' Oudit said, working the sharpened knife gently but deliberately into the carcass.

'Is tru tru Gaad, Oudit,' Rambarran said.

Slaughtering a sheep had been a communal thing. The whole barrack range took part, buying the sheep, then sharing the meat. Weddings, New Year and Phagwah were observed with pomp and gusto, as though everybody lived in one logie. Hindus and Muslims lived side by side, involved in each other's festivals. A Muslim male was secured whenever a Hindu wanted to slaughter a sheep. 'Fullah man hand make fo kill sheep,' Hindus would say. And the sheep's head was given to the Muslim who did the slaughtering.

'Nowadays things change,' added Rambarran. 'People turning like crab.'

'If you na lucky, you na get invitation to people wuk house, today,' Oudit remarked. 'Every man get sense since they living in this Scheme, in this high-house, eh. Fence-yard make them come like stranger.'

'And you na see how them lil boy growing up this time? Chu chu chu... they na get one ounce of manners. Wonda if pandit don't grind he teeth when he see them same lil boy mooma in mandir?' Rambarran's tone was full of regret. 'Wonda what going to happen to ahwe culture?' he asked, cutting deep into the carcass.

'Well-pipe in you yard, radio in you house, motor car pon road bring more disaster. True. Everybody come selfish. No closeness. Only pandit know the answer,' Oudit replied, remembering his promised jhandee. He needed to visit the pandit; he would tell him an auspicious time to hold it. At least, nobody could say me not upkeeping me religion. Is every six month me doing me jhandee. An' one time a year me wife doing she Durga Path. He consoled himself with these thoughts, believing one day he would be rewarded by Shree Bhagawan's beneficence. Me doing me duty, he told himself, helping himself to another snap.

It was still early in the morning. The men knew they had to finish cutting-up the meat, cleaning the intestines and washing them in time for the midday cooking.

'Married is a serious thing, beti,' Sumintra said solemnly, sitting on the edge of the bed. It was stifling in the bedroom. Data nodded, resting her head on a pillow. She wore a pinkish coloured dress, gold bangles and ear-rings. A spot of sindoor was visible in the middle of her long black hair. As she and Sumintra talked, her bashfulness gradually decreased. Girls and children still loitered in the sitting room, eager to have Data in their company. They joked, their excitement heightened by the dholak drumming coming from under the house.

'When you married is fo good. Not like how them black people living. And don't give you modin-law back answer. Shree Bhagawan would sin you.' Data smiled, nodding; she had heard this advice before.

'And talk-name is not good. Always hold you head in respect when you walk the street. And mind you own business. Tru, let people say you is one decent Hindu picknee. Not like some gal who going theatre three times every week. And giving they husband back answer pan top. Eh-eh, tink in ahwe days meself and you modin-law could do that? Never. Them ole people been straight like cane-arrow. Don't play with them culture... chu chu chu. Today some young people believe they fall pon tree top. No respect fo daddy and mooma. And cause they going to high school they tink they see sun befo them ole people. Eh-eh, going to mandir is not all. They must get Shree Bhagawan in they mind, day and night. Is not true, beti?' Sumintra added.

Data nodded, shifting in the bed. She recalled her mother's words: 'Never mind you na understand the Ganga puja an' the Durga Path. Never mind. Once you mind clean and you action pure, you bound to get blessing...'

'And you musn't mix-mix with them gal in the street,' Sumintra continued, 'They quick to throw bad name at you. And you know the *Gita* say is betta fo dead than to live in infamy...'

Sumintra sighed, and shifted her position, the urge for black tobacco gripping her. She felt a dryness in her throat, hunger gnawing her insides. She began smacking her lips, her dark-stained tongue rolling against them. Her eyes dilated as she tried to suppress the crawling sensation eating her stomach.

Data was taken aback. She got up, eyes bewildered. 'Is what happen, Nanny?'

'Nothing beti. Nothing. Is just me black tobacco. Me want chew some, but me lef it downstairs.'

'Oh,' Data sighed in relief, her face brightening. But Sumintra was under pressure. For the past two days her bowels seemed to be operating by their own volition. At unusual times, day or night, she farted, then had to visit the latrine. These irregularities started with a crawling sensation in her stomach. Is too much white rum, she cursed.

Now she was embarrassed. Suppose she farted? What would Data think? But she was conscious of Big-Bye mooma's command: 'Don't leave Data til me join you in the bedroom, you hear Sumintra?'

Sumintra contracted her bowels and shouted for one of the girls. A short, flat-nosed girl of fourteen hurried to the bedroom, eager to help, glancing at Data.

'Ask Big-Bye mooma to send up me tobacco, chile,' Sumintra said, inching further onto the bed. Is wonda what Big-Bye mooma doing so long downstairs, she asked herself, vowing not to touch an ounce of white rum when she did join the company.

By evening most of the guests were drunk, especially the men. The older men sang traditional Hindi songs and quoted verses from the *Ramayana*. The younger men sang Hindi film songs, lamenting that their favourite films were no longer being shown in the cinemas these days.

'When ahwe see film like *Saheed an Andaz,* ahwe feel like real Indian people. Ahwe Indian people great, you know...' one gaunt-looking middle-aged man said. He sat with four other men in a corner under the house, drinking and singing, their eyes reddened.

Big-Bye mooma and the women sported in the kitchen. They drank, danced, and teased each other. They exploded in lewd remarks everytime one of them began to dance, feet pounding, dress fluttering like an open umbrella.

'Oho oho...' the other women encouraged, clapping and commenting on the dancer's movements...

'Is true. You na hear them scientist in Merica had to study the *Gita* when they been making the bomb which kill them Japanese?' another man said, gulping down a drink.

'You damn well right,' a third man uttered. His scraggy face was sorrowful, his eyes meditative.

'Boy, ahwe Indian people could do a lot of things. Only thing is that ahwe na get the chance to get schooling. You tink them driva an overseer coulda play them ass with ahwe? Anyhow is good thing me learn Hindi, so me could read the book fo strengthen me faith else me been crack up...' the third man added.

Other groups of men huddled in separate corners, some drinking and singing, others arguing and drinking. As was his duty Big-Bye moved among them to ensure that no-one was short of food and drink. When satisfied that everyone was taken care of, he joined his friends. They were drinking, trying to act like big-men. They teased Big-Bye.

'Don't take the stuff too much. Tonight is you big night.'

Big-Bye's heart skipped a beat. He had not taken too much alcohol. He knew. He was still imagining how Data would look when they went to bed. He was too ashamed to tell his friends he had never experienced sexual intercourse.

'Anyhow, take it cool, man,' another friend said, laughing and clapping Big-Bye on the shoulder. He urged the others to drink. Afterwards, conversations centred around girls and women.

FIVE

By seven o' clock Data had already bathed and changed, liberally rubbing powder on her armpits and body. She was not afraid. She knew marriage involved sexual intercourse, though she had little idea what the experience would be like. 'Once you born a girl child you gat to get married,' her mother had always warned. She accepted that statement unquestioningly, regarding sex as another wifely duty.

Big-Bye, too, had bathed and changed, taking extra care to brush his teeth clean. He didn't want his breath to smell of alcohol. He knew kissing was involved, though when his friends had talked about tongue-kissing a woman he was not quite sure what they meant. As he bathed, his penis hardened. He wondered if the act would be the same as the one he attempted years ago with the little girls in the fowl-pen. He flushed at the memory, the pleasure of the game and the shame of being discovered. It go be sweet, he told himself, throwing water on his skin, feeling elevated, a sense of power in his erection

By the time he had taken dinner, the guests had already left, only Sumintra and his mooma remaining. He could hear their voices deep in conversation in the kitchen. Big-Bye papa was snoring in the bedroom.

'You make sure the sheet spread on the bed?' Big-Bye mooma asked, concerned.

'Me make sure the sheet spread end to end,' Sumintra answered. 'An me tell doolahin not to trouble the sheet. Me say that is holy sheet, an it have to spread on the bed tonight. She understand.'

Big-Bye mooma clucked her tongue mischievously, reflecting on her own second Sunday night. How me been stoopid, she told herself. At least me modin-law could never say me eye black...

An hour later Big-Bye and Data locked themselves in his bedroom. At long last Sumintra had been able to go after saying goodnight to Data; she was longing to rest her old feet at home. She hoped that when morning came, the bedsheet would prove Data's virginity. Only that would satisfy Big-Bye mooma.

Around nine, quietness fell on the village, broken only by dogs barking and the voices of the youths, seemingly anchored for the night at the street ends, exploding in laughter. The electric lights were off in most of the houses. An occasional gust of wind rattled zinc sheets, stirring leaves and flowers.

Big-Bye mooma rolled in bed, sighed, focusing her ears on Big-Bye's bedroom. There was silence in the house, disturbed only by Big-Bye papa's snoring and occasional muffled groan. A sudden commotion caught her attention, but she decided it must be cats rummaging in the backyard when she heard them mewing at each other.

Big-Bye fingered Data's nightdress awkwardly, mumbling words of love. His heart beat faster, gripped by an unbearable expectancy, wondering if his mooma was asleep. He could smell Data's elusive but powerful womanliness. There was no way he could hold back the hunger which gnawed at him.

Data lay quietly, but her breathing grew louder as she felt a sweet sensation as Big-Bye's fingers roamed her breast and abdomen, hungry to peel off her panties. Data wondered if Big-Bye had ever experienced sex. She couldn't read his actions. He was clumsy, acting as though he wanted to crush her.

She remained passive, but a feeling of heat from her thighs and nipples spread through her body.

As Big-Bye's fingers stroked her thick pubic hair, she began to feel pleasure, eyes closed, her breathing coming distinct, her nipples erect.

Then Big-Bye took off his shorts hurriedly and climbed on top of her, parting her thighs with his hands. As Big-Bye tried to penetrate, he gripped her roughly, thrusting down his penis to find an entry.

Data clenched her teeth, emitting muffled sobs, feeling the hardened penis hitting with force against her still dry vulva.

'Open you leg more na girl,' Big-Bye said affectionately, wanting to get into Data. His hunger felt uncontrollable. He forgot about kissing.

Data opened her thighs wider, trying not to feel the hurt. If only she had understood properly when her friend Sandra had told her 'it hurt bad-bad the first time,' she would have annointed her inside with coconut oil. She had heard of newly married girls who used coconut oil on their parts in preparation for the second Sunday night, but she never questioned which part had to be annointed. She was ashamed to ask. No proper Hindu girl asked such questions, the seamstress had said one morning. The apprentice-girls giggled.

'According to de book, marriage is a discovery. As you live together de man and wife learn more,' the seamstress added. She had been married for over ten years.

Data thought about these words as Big-Bye struggled to penetrate her. Her inside was tight. She tried to suppress the burning pain she felt, tears streaming down her cheeks.

'Ouch! O Gaad!' she blurted out, feeling something tear inside her as Big-Bye's penis sank into her suddenly. Then he clutched at her and she felt a sudden shudder and a spurt of warmth. Then it was all over as he pulled himself out of her and slumped beside her.

In the adjoining bedroom Big-Bye mooma turned in bed, alerted by Data's cry of pain. She wished the morning would break early, curious to examine the bedsheet.

'Never could trust,' she mumbled quietly, willing herself to sleep.

Data felt a warm trickling oozing from inside her. There had been more pain than ecstacy.

Big-Bye felt a tremendous relief. He lay beside Data, breathing quietly, his hands resting on her breast. He felt a burning at the tip of his penis.

An hour later both were asleep.

Big-Bye and Data woke before six the next morning. Big-Bye wanted to make love. He played with Data, stroking her face, breasts and legs, exploring her body in curiosity. He felt exhilarated as he cupped her breast. His desire was uncontrollable. Data complained, moaned in pain as Big-Bye tried to enter her, but his urge was greater than any awareness of what she suffered.

He felt the warmth in Data's inside as he pushed, but he had no sense of how she felt. Data wanted to push him off. The pain was too much. But it was her duty. She gritted her teeth. She wished Big-Bye would stop. Big-Bye clasped her, moaned, then ejaculated. He felt good, breathing slower and telling himself: Data sweet. I like fucking she...

As soon as Data and Big-Bye emerged from the bedroom and went downstairs to wash, Big-Bye mooma hurriedly entered their bedroom. Her steps were nimble, actions stealthy. The room was disarranged, clothes thrown here and there, drawers in the wardrobe open. She stood beside the bed, eyeing the crumpled white sheet. Her eyes searched, then she sighed in satisfaction as she saw drops of blood on the sheet, dry, coated by a jellyish stain.

'At least me na get one second-hand doolahin in me house,' she said, feeling released. 'Me know me choose one good wife fo Big-Bye. Tru. Whenever me na able do puja, me doolahin going do it. And she mind pure like rainwater.'

'Doolahin,' she shouted, voice choked with satisfaction, as she entered the downstairs kitchen. She began directing the morning chores, her steps rapid, her voice now coated in honey. She rummaged among the utensils, instructing Data to start the chulafire. 'Take you time, doolahin. The marning young. Big-Bye papa and Big-Bye not going backdam today.'

Data obeyed, hurrying to set the pots on the chula-fireside. She wanted her mother-in-law to know she could work efficiently in the kitchen. Occasionally she bit her tongue, trying to suppress the burning sensation she felt in her vagina.

After telling Data what to cook, Big-Bye mooma went out to the bottom-house with a coconut-branch broom. Gat to know if she could cook, she told herself. Is no use you faithful and you can't cook. Befo me jump-in fourteen, me coulda cook, wash and run house, never mind me na get good schooling... Tru. Now is different time...

She bubbled in happiness as she swept the bottom-house. She wanted to show Sumintra the sheet, but decided to do so only after showing Data.

As she continued sweeping, brooming the dust towards one corner of the yard, she planned how the house-work should be divided between herself and Data. Is time now to get some rest, she thought; she would handle the lighter tasks but must not burden Data too much.

Outside, naked children and grown-up youths loitered on the rolled, red-brick road. They frolicked, quarrelled, some reluctant, some afraid to make their way to the wooden, two-storey, school building about fifty rods away from the back street. Mothers shouted warnings from inside their yards, aware that it was nearing eight in the morning. Men and women engaged in the provision and fish businesses passed each other, going their different ways. Sugar workers had already gone to the canefields long before the day opened, working bags and cutlasses slung across their shoulders. It was a bright morning; dogs barked, donkeys brayed beyond the street-head, fowls cackled – sounds carried further by the gusting wind.

'Come see this ting, doolahin,' Big-Bye mooma said, directing Data's eyes to the bloodstained sheet.

Data halted by the bedroom doorway, glimpsed the dry blood on the sheet, and hung her head in shame.

'Nothing to be shame about, doolahin,' Big-Bye mooma said affectionately. 'It show that you decent. That you come from a proper Hindu home. That you parents is strict. Me always believe a proper Hindu gal should keep she self fo she husband. She must be one Sita, the light in she husband eye.' She smiled, folding the sheet reverently, lamenting all the while the attitudes and behaviour of some of the girls in the village.

'Them is disgrace to ahwe religion. They only going to mandir fo show-off. True. They burning diva and hearing jhandee to show people. But is shaitan in they mind. If you hear how they name stinking? Chu chu chu... tink this eye-pass coulda happen in ahwe time? Is chaacha and chachee, and uncle and auntie to everybody who more big than you. Never mind living been hard in Estate, but ahwe had better religion,' she added.

Suddenly she raised her head, aware that Data was still there. She smiled and said: 'Go see after kitchen. Me going make up bed, and clean bedroom.'

'Yes Ma,' Data replied, walking away, wondering what Big-Bye mooma would do with the blood-stained sheet. She felt ashamed and a little offended that her mother-in-law had needed proof of her virginity. She had heard of similar cases where mothers-in-law tested their sons' wives chastity, but had not known the method. Yet, as she washed the cooking utensils in the wooden kitchen sink, watching the water drain through a small gutter into the backyard pond used to water the plants grown there, she felt clean. At least Big-Bye mooma could never point her finger, tell her to rub blackpot on her face or call her a whore. She knew she could walk anywhere with head held high. She felt satisfaction and pride, and decided to offer milk at the altar after doing her next Sunday morning puja. She would live cordially with Big-Bye mooma, show her all due respect. 'Once you live good wid you modin-law, Shree Bhagawan going always bless you. She is like you second mooma.' Data knew that her mother's words made good sense. She smiled contentedly, coating her fingers with soapsuds, surveying the backyard. There were rows of well-cared for calaloo, boulanger and peppers. She noted the well-set drainage and recalled her father's vegetable plot aback their house. Her father loved his plants, his one-acre ricefield and his two cows. Many evenings, observing him working in the back garden, she noted how calm and yet commanding his actions were, the plants under the gentle subjection of his fingers, a compassionate understanding in his eyes. He often left the garden only when darkness descended amidst the croakings of frogs, the chirrupings of beetles and crickets.

Curious to know why he treated the plants so lovingly, she asked one evening: 'But, Daddy, is why you treating them plants as if them is eggs?'

'Aha beti,' her father said. He was eating a dinner of dal, rice, bhoonjal shrimp, with a sprinkling of tamarind achaar. He sat on a low wooden bench, between the doorway of the well-daubed, earthen-floored kitchen. A lighted kerosene lamp resting on a wooden shelf flickered; faint shadows danced on the crusted wallboards every time the wind blew.

She sat on another low wooden bench, dressed in a loose, flowered cotton dress, long black hair hanging free. It was silent outside.

'Beti, me feel free in de garden. Me could express me real self when me hold these plants. Is like when me praying in de mandir. Me could talk to Shree Bhagawan just how me talking to them plants,' her father explained. Then he assumed a solemn look, his facial muscles strained as if in pain, wrinkles visible. 'But is different in de backdam. You

56

never know you true self. Me been working so long in de field, and me still is one stranger between them cane. Never get one chance fo them understand me. But is different in me own garden. Different in de mandir.'

Looking at this back garden now, she was sure the same affinity existed between its plants and the gardener as existed in her father's garden. Funny way to feel, she thought, drying the utensils with a white hand-towel, wondering what Big-Bye mooma would like to cook for the midday meal.

Big-Bye had gone out after the morning meal, telling Data: 'Me going to see them boys on the road.' He smiled at her, his eyes wanting to show he really preferred being with her, but he knew that if he hung around her, his mooma would believe he liked Data more than she. Big-Bye papa, feeling worn-out, as though he had worked for days without taking a rest, had told his wife that he would be visiting Dalmohan who had said he wanted to sell his provision plot. Big-Bye papa thought it a good investment and wanted to seal the bargain that day.

'Me na able wuk land, Loknauth,' Dalmohan had said. 'Me wuk land since me lil boy. An me na get no satisfaction. Me feel empty inside. Is time fo me devote me ole days to Gaad. Befo me dead me going feel happy...'

His tone had wracked Loknauth like the bite of a cane-scorpion. His pained expression, his scraggy face, fleshless frame, stiff joints, reflected Loknauth's feelings about the monotony of his own life.

They had sat on a bench under Dalmohan's bottom-house. Children were playing outside. The usual barrage of voices in the wind as evening meals were being prepared on chula-fires in neighbouring houses.

Both men sat like emblems of patience, absorbed in concern over the uncertainty of their tomorrows, seeing their world of sacred ceremonies threatened by creole ways.

'Is de same, Loknauth,' Dalmohan added. 'Dis high house na make no difference at all. Ahwe still want to know, to understand ahwe true self. What is de purpose of ahwe life? Is not only wukkin, eatin, drinkin. No. Is something else.'

Loknauth nodded. He, too, often felt a similar agony. Felt moments of happiness only when he was involved in the religious festivals or lost in sessions of rum-fired reminiscence. During such times his agony would be muffled and he would find expression in Hindi bhajans, though still baffled by the karma of his existence. There was no respite. Was it his fate to trudge incessantly between his home, the sugarcane fields, the back garden and the temple? Was his destiny pre-ordained? 'Suppose me been born in one next country?' he often asked himself, slumped on his bed as if needing a long rest. 'Me na believe me life woulda be so empty... Me shoulda take schooling...'

At first Loknauth wanted to withdraw from the offer he had made for the plot. Like Dalmohan, he, too, wanted to devote himself to God, to find his true self, but his wife had said: 'You only have two more years fo serve the Estate. Tink if the pension money could feed you. When you get land, you get food in you belly. When you na able, Big-Bye going work it.'

Loknauth saw the sense in his wife's advice. He could always count on Big-Bye. After his death the land would fall in Big-Bye's hand, but Dalmohan had nobody to work the land. Since the death of his wife five years ago, he had turned his back on his daughters.

'They just like blackman. They eatin pork an beef. They going birthnight. Chu chu. When good-day come they drinkin daro. An they na get altar in they yard. Eh-eh, them is shaitan. Not even one cup pani me want drink in they kitchen...'

Dalmohan wanted to sell the land for seven hundred dollars, including the growing crops of yams, dasheen, cassava and plantains. 'Me going do one katha. Den me going to mandir everyday,' he said when Loknauth was leaving. He saw himself in front of the temple-altar, the garlanded images smiling at him, lost in contemplation, transcended in the abode of Vrindabhan... Lord Krishna's kingdom. 'Is then me going to have peace,' he whispered.

Loknauth bought the land.

Later in the day Big-Bye mooma placed the bloodstained sheet in a drawer in the polished, mahogony dressing table in her own bedroom. 'Me have to show Sumintra,' she vowed, and began dusting her bedroom. If every modin-law been stay like me, tink datin-law coulda give them modin-law hot-mouth? Never the day, she told herself, sighing.

Was different in ahwe time. True. Today young people not even care to shave them picknee head. Them not even want do nine-day. They want turn Christain, walking with bible all about the place, calling Jesus Christ the son of Gad. What about Shiva? Lord Krishna? Stoopid people. Gaad ever get son. Is this Christain bottom-house corrupting them young people. Is what salvation they could get if they not keeping up nine-day an katha an jhandee. Go throw picknee hair in Ganga mata. Aha, them was real shave-head wuk. Her dark-ringed eyes brightened and a lightness invaded her body as she recalled a particular shave-head ceremony held years back. Yet there was, too, a momentary pang of half-remembered grief...

She was about seventeen, living in a two bedroom logie with Loknauth and his parents. Her first child, a girl, had died a couple of weeks before during an outbreak of malaria which had claimed the lives of many babies. In the Nigger Yard where they lived, there was no proper system of drainage and malaria-carrying mosquitoes thrived in the insanitary morass of mud and excrement which made a misery of the workers' lives during the rainy season. Such deaths were all too common then and she had overcome her grief and resumed work in the weeding gang.

Spirits lifted as the sugar workers living in the barrack

ranges and nearby cottages sensed that rainy season was coming to an end. Uplift turned to excitement when the news spread that a shave-head ceremony was to be held the coming Sunday morning. It was for Rajpattie's second child, born nine months ago, spared from the malarial scourge.

'Lucky picknee,' people said. Rajpattie lived in the same barrack range occupied by Big-Bye mooma. From Saturday evening the men began constructing the bamboo tent in front of the logie, laughing and cracking jokes, contemplating tomorrow's feast.

Big-Bye mooma and other women were inside Rajpattie's logie. Some peesayed gera, dye and garlic on a masala brick, others sliced pumpkins, potatoes and calaloo. A group of young girls changed the window blinds and decorated the walls with coloured rice, pasting them in geometric designs.

They worked with a singular absorption and energy, as if they were the focus of the coming ceremony and Rajpattie and her child were mere participants. They laughed and joked, sweat crowning their brows and armpits, the older women directing the chores, the younger ones obeying: 'Yes chaachee. Eh-eh, auntie.'

As the preparations ran into the night, the drummers and singers came – a group of five old women and men, versed in the bhajans that were sung on such occasions. They were devoted temple worshippers and most could speak Hindi, even if it was a little from memory and unconfidently.

The entertainers sat in a privileged corner under the rusted aluminium awning of the logie. Kerosene lanterns flickered as men and women moved about, happiness in their hearts, glad to undertake whatever task was given them. Fireflies veered, sparked, went out and reappeared in the surrounding darkness.

As the bhajans flowed, stirred by the accelerating tempo of the drum, a chorus of uninhibited happiness, of dancing and laughter pervaded the yard. Each individual sensed that his or her presence took on meaning as part of a collective statement; each grasped as something living and still whole in the tradition they were proud to call their own.

The singing and dancing lasted far into the night, the hours measured only by the crowing of the cocks.

The next morning as the sun peeped golden through the crevices between the rolling clouds, breaking the shroud of dawn, Big-Bye mooma and the other women were waiting in Rajpattie's logie. They had already bathed from the wooden ghats along the edge of the black water canal behind the barrack ranges. The water was cool and dark when the women, using a half-calabash, dipped water from the canal to douse themselves. Further along its banks, old dhoti-clad men hummed Hindi mantras as they offered white and red oleanders to the water.

Then the drummers came to Rajpattie's yard, the drum-cracks calling the women to form up in procession. Most of them wore white cotton dresses, white orhnis tucked on their heads, hands and feet enhanced by decorative silver jewellery. As they followed the drummers, pandit, and singers out of Rajpattie's yard, out of the Nigger Yard, onto the dusty dam, their faces were solemn, awe and reverence in their every footfall on the redbrick road snaking to the beach. Rajpattie's child was carried by her mother-in-law, a stoutish, fair-skin woman, proud that every part of the ceremony followed the instructions handed down by their elders.

On the shell-strewn beach the pandit, dhoti-clad, took over. While the drummers heated their drum-skins in front of a fire, the shave-head ceremony began a couple of yards away on the sand. Camphor and agarbatti were lit. A split dry coconut and mango leaves were placed in a circle drawn on the beach by the pandit. A little fire burnt in the centre, exuding the fragrance of sandalwood and ghee. As the pandit conducted the ceremony, quoting from the *Puranas,* the women, tight-lipped, absorbed, were drawn further into the ritual until, their fervour rising, their spirits entered the presence of the gods, worshipped and worshippers becoming one.

As everyone broke into Shantih, Shantih, the pandit beckoned the child. He prayed over her, sprinkling water from a brass-cup. Then he directed the barber to shave off the child's hair, giving instructions to Rajpattie and another woman how to scoop up the burnt materials used in the ceremony. When they had done that, the women walked to the edge of the sea and threw their votive offering into the water. For them this seashore was the river Ganges, as it was for the other groups conducting similar ceremonies and pujas all along the beach front.

When he had instructed Rajpattie's mother-in-law and the other women what to do, the pandit hurried off to conduct another ceremony being held not far away.

The shaven hair was thrown in the sea-water, the women mumbling Hindi mantras, then the child was submerged in the water seven times, invoking Ganga's spirit to sanctify the baptism.

Then the women called on Ganga to grant them health and happiness, to grant children to those without and to forgive those who had sinned. After this they felt renewed, humming mantras as they changed. All the way back to the logie they sang and danced, their steps moving to the rhythm of the drumbeats, a joyful procession, a procession which led all the way back to the traditions of their ancestors.

In the logie and in the bamboo tent everyone feasted on the cooked rice and vegetables, their tongues blazed by the hot mango achaar. They belched in satisfaction, rubbing their bellies. Some who had eaten too much slumped in corners. Little boys frequented the beezie-beezie bush, aback the barrack ranges, emptying their bowels, planning to eat again.

Rajpattie's child, all the time being passed from hand to hand, was offered gifts of money, gold jewels and pieces of clothing by the guests.

The singing, dancing, eating and drinking lasted until nightfall. By then everyone was tired but satisfied that a sacred obligation had been fulfilled.

'Aih, Big-Bye mooma,' Sumintra called, her walking stick tapping as she entered the yard.

Big-Bye mooma snapped into the present, annoyed by Sumintra's sudden intrusion. She hurried to finish her work in the bedroom, trying to recall when last she had attended such a shave-head ceremony since living in this housing scheme. She wished young people could see the meaning of their culture, visit the mandir more often. This bottom-house clap-hand church, hallelujah singing, Sunday school service was no fit culture for Hindu people. Then she recalled the bloodstained sheet and her eyes glinted with satisfaction. She knew she had scored a point over Sumintra.

SIX

Big-Bye and Data retired to bed early the following night. Big-Bye couldn't contain his lust, as though gripped by a desire suppressed for years. Data was pleased that Big-Bye evidently liked her, even though he was clumsy and had hurt her. And when he had touched her body gently, she had begun to feel that there might be some pleasure in the act. However, it was her duty as a wife to please him, so she said nothing to him about her own feelings.

'Take off the light,' she told him, abashed, as he took off his clothes, revealing a very visible erection pressing against his briefs. She wore a loose cotton nightdress, and smelt of powder. 'Husband like when you smell sweet,' women said.

In bed Big-Bye fumbled at Data's breasts, his lust rising.

'Don't hurry. Me thing still hurting,' Data whispered.

'Girl, me really want you thing,' he whispered, trying to contain the heat in his groin before it exploded. With one hand he cupped Data's right breast, stroking the nipple, with the fingers of the other hand he caressed her pubic mound. Data felt herself opening and growing moist, the desire becoming irresistible. As Big-Bye mounted her, her breath grew rapid, rising and falling in spasms.

It was quiet in the house. Big-Bye mooma and papa were outside, talking. The night was dark and a heavy wind blew, rattling zinc sheets and rustling the fruit trees growing in the backyards.

Big-Bye's penetration hurt.

Ouch ouch... Data moaned, teeth clenched, thighs stiffened, hands on Big-Bye's back. Big-Bye's desire increased, the ecstacy rising; he groaned with pleasure. Then he ejaculated, feeling deep release.

Data was left on the edge of satisfaction, without release. She sighed, muffling her disgust, feeling the distaste of the act in her saliva. Maybe she would enjoy it the next time, she told herself. It wouldn't pain so much.

'The thing sweet,' Big-Bye whispered in her ear, caressing her flat abdomen.

Data preferred to remain quiet, immersed in her own thoughts. She could not see herself as a married woman yet.

'Girl, me never know you thing been so sweet,' Big-Bye added, saying he wished he didn't have to cut cane in the morning, that he wanted to be with her.

'The work does be hard sometime.' The years of canefield work ahead, like a life sentence, suddenly yawned in front of him. He had witnessed too many men age quickly, turning sickly, suffering terrible backaches and stiffened joints. Some complained of suffering insomnia, others of a weakened manhood.

'If you ain't get guts, you ain't able wid backdam wuk,' sugar workers would say, praying that they would not fall ill. 'You back must be strong to cut cane.' 'De compensation money not anything dis time. Den Dispensary not getting proper medicine. Is only faith gat to keep you alive.' These were the remarks Big-Bye heard at wedding-houses and wake-houses. And whenever his papa complained of backache and stiffened joints, asking his mooma to massage him before he went to bed, he saw a future he had to avoid.

'Estate work ain't get a future,' he told himself, cursing his fate, wondering why he couldn't take education, unlike Doodnauth, his schoolmate. Big-Bye nudged Data. 'Ow,' she sighed, rubbing his chest, still thinking. Big-Bye decided not to talk, just caress her stomach.

Yes! Doodnauth. They had been classmates together. Doodnauth was brilliant. 'Dood head make to take eddication,' boys in the class said with envy.

Doodnauth was given special privileges by each class teacher. He was forgiven for coming late to school. He cut tamarind rods for the teachers, he kept the class whenever that particular class-teacher was out. He helped to hold the hands of the boys being whipped. The boys in his class feared, respected and sometimes loathed him. He was the darling of the girls. Some middays he would be found behind the school latrine, caressing either Shamdai or Kairul, the two girls who most desired his attention.

During all these happenings Big-Bye was Doodnauth's closest companion. Yet, Big-Bye couldn't fathom the secret of Doodnauth's brilliance, except to believe he had been made that way.

'Some picknee head just fit fo take schooling,' his mooma would remark at the end of the school-year when Big-Bye's poor examination results were known.

'Is Shree Bhagawan wuk. What ever he will fo you in you past janam, must happen in this janam,' his mooma added, her smile expressing a contented bafflement with life, her eyes brooding on its mystery.

Remarks such as these undermined Big-Bye's confidence and motivation, and although Headmaster Bryan constantly drummed in the students' ears: 'Only education can give you equality, and make you a man in this society,' how to put these words into practice slipped Big-Bye's understanding like water through open fingers.

Yet he knew what privileges education offered. He envied Doodnauth especially when, lurking behind a clump of beezie-beezie tom-peeping, he saw him either with Shamdai or Kairul. Sometimes he caught Doodnauth with his fingers tickling the girls' underdeveloped nipples or trying to broach their panties.

And whenever the class teacher summoned Doodnauth

to the front of the class, telling him to work out the multiplication on the blackboard so the 'nit-heads' could see, Big-Bye felt his own intelligence insulted. Why couldn't it be him? But he knew what a fool he would become if placed in front of the class to work out the answer.

On other days he envied the young, Black teachers, dressed in clean white shirts, tie, and black pants, each student calling them Sir. Them head, too, been make fo take schooling? Maybe, them must do something good in them past janam.

This conflict, between what he wanted and what he feared he could never achieve, followed him from class to class. Each year he barely made the pass marks. He wanted to know when the conflict would end.

One midday sitting under the tamarind tree in the school yard, he explained his dilemma to Doodnauth.

'Is you mooma and papa, Big-Bye,' Doodnauth said. 'They don't care. But every night me own papa asking me what teacher learn me in school. If is sums, me have to work them out, then show he. If is tables, me have to repeat it, and learn he. If me only refuse, is cut-rass. And me papa don't make sport when he beating you. Boy, Big-Bye, some night me does want runaway in the beezie-beezie bush.'

Big-Bye tried to imagine Doodnauth's pain. Now he understood the sadness which clouded Doodnauth's face as they trekked home along the redbrick road from school in the sunbright afternoons.

'One Saturday afternoon me grandpapa tell me that me own papa been swear and say, that me gat to take eddication, else he is no man,' Doodnauth said as they crossed the wooden-bridge and took the road that led to the village.

Doodnauth had looked worried as they walked the dusty dam to their respective homes. He added: 'Me papa been tell me in front me mooma one night, that eddication could make you equal with overseer and book-keeper. And the more you get eddication is better favour you getting from

Manager. And that he gat to see me take eddication, else he murder me...'

By the time Doodnauth reached the Sixth Standard, Big-Bye and many other students had dropped out of school because of their low marks. Big-Bye was fourteen. At first he had felt an immense sense of release from existing always on the edge of failure and humiliation. He had discovered that there was a world where he could be somebody and though Big-Bye mooma insisted that he learnt tailoring, Big-Bye was attracted to the canefields.

'Is how you like Joe mule? It shine, an it could gallop.'

'What yuh tink bout Irene? Gaad. She ain't get shame. She fucking with Sambo driver in de canefield. I does proper give she a fat-eye...'

'An you don't talk how you peeping dem weeder when dem crossing de canal. An you feeling you iron, an pump out de spence when you see you mule cock stand up. Heh heh...'

Statements like these spiced street-corner conversations, or when the mule-boys got together in a corner at a wake-house. Big-Bye would hang around them, listening. Their talk suggested a romantic, intriguing world of adventure and independence. He wanted to hear more. Whenever he spotted the mule-boys sitting at the street-corners, on bright evenings, playing cards, he sneaked out of his yard and lingered among them. He felt useful and accepted whenever one of them sent him to buy cigarettes.

'Sit down an watch how big men does play card,' one of the mule-boys would tell him. His eyes would be glued to their every mannerism, how they smoked, cursed and drank like big men.

Some evenings the mule-boys would argue, comparing horses and gun-toting movie-stars from the American Westerns. Their judgements seemed so assured, their knowledge so wide. Big-Bye wished he could join them when they went to the cinema in Buxton on Saturday nights, or got drunk at wedding-houses in the village.

One Saturday evening Big-Bye plucked up the courage to ask his mooma's permission to go and see a movie with the mule-boys. The attraction was great. 'Is two powerful cowboy films. Is there you going see man draw gun...' the mule-boys had said with boisterous excitement and much dumb-show.

'Not one bit!' his mooma snapped, face contorted in passion. 'Think that is ahwe culture? Soontime me going hear you eating black pudding and souse. You must see Hindi film never mind you na understand the talking. Beside, them devtas inside Hindi film. You hear me? You going to see how to pray. How to respect ole people...'

Big-Bye never again asked his mooma's permission to visit the cinema, but he found various excuses to stay away from home on many evenings.

By the time Doodnauth gained the College of Preceptors certificate, Big-Bye was a regular member of the mule-boys group. Some nights he sneaked out of the house, unknown to his parents, and visited the cinema in their company. And the more he was with them, the less he could resist the call of the canefields. The pictures they painted dwelled in his imagination indelibly.

'Boy, if you see dem weeding woman leg, eh-eh...'

'Some ah dem must be really get bush pon dem cat, eh...'

'I want put a cock in Unis. She rass like wine-up she backside too much, boy. When she weeding by Dam-bed, am me passing wid me mule, an she see me, eh-eh, if you see how she making up she eye. You going to believe she tun sakiwinkee.'

'I tink she want you, Bissoon. Why you ain't clap one good cock pon she?'

'Boy Ranjit, when you gallop you mule you like real starboy. Eh-eh, is only de gun you need.'

'You tink you able with backdam?' Big-Bye mooma barked at him one mid-week night, eyes ferocious, hands akimbo. They were under the house alone. Big-Bye papa had gone out to attend a wake for Old Man Bhola.

Big-Bye had just announced that he was joining the mule-gang. He claimed his head couldn't take to tailoring.

'You going sorry, Big-Bye,' she warned, crestfallen, feeling a chill in her body. Her son's declaration had come at the same time as Bhola's death. She recalled that a jumbie bird had flown across the house two dark nights before, hooting three times and the dogs had cried in the street. The following night Bhola died. Bad times were ahead, she concluded. And now Big-Bye. Canefield! Is a warning. She had seen too much suffering from canefield work. She knew about the frequent miscarriages in the weeding gangs when pregnant women had fallen in the wet, slippery fields... the faces of the drivers unmoved, hardened like the sun-baked earth which blunted the edges of shovels... And now Big-Bye.

But Big-Bye was determined, adopting a no-compromise posture he had copied from one of the mule-boys.

'Me son, Big-Bye, me make you, and me know what is good fo you. You going sorry. Me might not live to see, but you going always remember me words. It would never drop in water...' Big- Bye mooma said in pity. She decided to do more praying. Begged Shree Bhagawan to make her son's working conditions in the fields less harsh, to help him find favour in the drivers' and overseers' eyes.

When Big-Bye did join the mule-gang at the age of sixteen, Doodnauth was taking book-keeping lessons from a retired book-keeper called Singh, an embittered, hard-drinking man who regularly cursed: 'Why me couldn't become Manager? Know I could read and write more than all of them. Cause me is a coolie man?' Nevertheless, Singh was an assiduous teacher.

At first Big-Bye and Doodnauth still met on the street corners but their former closeness had gone. Gradually the boys drifted apart, each seeking his own destiny. Doodnauth became a clerk at Enmore Estate Pay office, about four miles from the village, and Big-Bye had graduated from mules to the canecutting gang.

By the time Big-Bye jolted back to awareness, Data was snoring, one hand resting on his chest. He felt drawn to her. Out of curiosity, he pulled up her nightdress cautiously, and began caressing her inner thighs, moving stealthily towards her pubic hair. Gaad, this woman pussy fat and high, he told himself, aware of his hardening penis. Pussy high like cane-bed...

Data shifted, turned and groaned. 'Leh me sleep na.'

Big-Bye drew away his fingers guiltily, heart beating fast. He sensed she felt he was taking a liberty with her and settled for nestling close, his fingers on her breast. Shit, this woman leg smooth like trench water, he told himself and tried to sleep. Why me couldn't take-in eddication?

SEVEN

A week later Data still felt like a stranger. She longed to spend a day at her mother's home. It was not that her mother-in-law ever treated her unkindly; indeed, during the day they partnered the house-work: sweeping, washing, cooking, going to the market. But it was not like being with her own mother. All the same, she listened dutifully to the advice given her by Big-Bye mooma.

'Must always keep the place clean,' Big-Bye mooma had insisted on the fourth morning after the second Sunday. They were under the house. Big-Bye and his papa had gone to the canefields early in the morning.

'When people come they must see how clean the place is. Not like some people place which look like pig-pen, who cooking pork and beef in the same pot in which they cooking sweet-rice and methai... chu chu, them like real caprinyah,' Big-Bye mooma added, cringing her nose.

After taking the midday meal they would lounge under the house, Big-Bye mooma lying in the hammock, Data sitting nearby on an open sugarsack spread on the ground.

'You getting breeze here,' Big-Bye mooma would say, inhaling draughts of air. She felt it was time to relax her old bones.

Data would search Big-Bye mooma's long, grey hair for lice, killing them with a plop between her fingernails. Then she would comb it. Big-Bye mooma would sigh with pleasure, though her eyes would dart at passers-by, particularly young girls traipsing their way to the market in the main street. She would pout her lips and smack her tongue, saying, 'Look how them young girls dress. Eh-eh, they feel they going Gargetown. They should wear long dress.'

Hearing such remarks Data would smile, though not in Big-Bye mooma's sight. They get a right to dress the way they feel, she would say silently, admiring the girls' dresses.

When Data realised Big-Bye mooma wanted to sleep she would go upstairs to her room where she would try to sleep, but could think of nothing other than her urge to visit her mother. However, she knew that such a visit could bring rumours. People in her village would say, 'Eh-eh, look like she and she husband get teeth and tongue. Tikkay she husband ain't find she good.' She consoled herself with the knowledge that in three weeks time she would be able to visit her mother and nobody could say anything then.

Later in the afternoon, after rising with a puffy face, she would begin preparing the evening meal of boiled split-peas, rice, calaloo, fried shrimp, followed by coconut achaar. As the afternoon dimmed, Big-Bye papa, when he had eaten his evening meal, would tend the back garden. Big-Bye mooma looked after the chickens. Data washed the wares after they had taken dinner and then she would prepare tea or crushed plantain porridge. Big-Bye, meantime, would make a quick visit to the street-corners. Now he felt he was really a married man, though he didn't spend very long with the boys before returning home. But he couldn't let his friends think that married life had made him a slave. 'Eh-eh, like he never see woman yet,' they would say. 'Like Data the only woman in the world.'

To this daily routine of chores and family habits, Data had adjusted herself by the end of the first week. She knew what to do, what to expect. Yet she could not yet feel that she really belonged or counted there.

One Tuesday morning in the second week, old man Lalo, who lived in the back street, walked into the yard, tapping his walking stick on the concrete pathway that led into the bottom-house. Big-Bye mooma and Sumintra sat under the house, discussing Cinthi's funeral, saying what a good woman this Cinthi had been.

Data was in the downstairs kitchen sifting rice. She sat on a chair, the rice spread out on the table, her fingers separating the husk from the grain. On the two previous mid-week afternoons she had glued her ears to Big-Bye mooma's and Sumintra's conversation. Their talk had centred around people living in the village, about their characters, the good and bad of them. Data wanted to know why Big-Bye mooma and Sumintra pulled people apart in that way, laughing heh heh heh, as if deriving a special pleasure from doing it.

Seeing Lalo now, Data expected to hear more conversation of this kind, so as she sifted the rice, she focused her ears under the house.

'Hay, Lalo bhai, is where you been?' Big-Bye mooma greeted Lalo pleasantly, inviting him to a small bench near the hammock.

Lalo took his time, the bones in his body cracking as he sat down. His hands faltered, his fingers trembled; wrinkled flesh hung loosely on his body. He was balding; only his piercing eyes suggested the man he had once been.

'Bhai Lalo, you eat food this marning?' Sumintra asked, rolling black tobacco in her palms.

'Yes, Didi,' Lalo mumbled. He knew he would eat lunch here. Big-Bye mooma and Sumintra always treated him as though he was their own brother.

'Bhai Lalo, you been Cinthi wake-house?' Big-Bye mooma asked curiously. She knew Lalo was present at every wake-house and funeral, at every wedding-house and jhandee held in the village.

Lalo shook his head disappointly. 'Wake-house na go nice. Young boys gambling downstairs an drink daro. Picknee dry cry, an burn candle. Ting na go right...'

'And me tell them. Cinthi is born Hindu,' Sumintra

added. 'What right picknee gat to burn candle? Cause them turn Christain?'

'O Shree Bhagawan!' Big-Bye mooma exclaimed, eyes dilated in fear. 'Cinthi not going rest in peace. She spirit going haunt the house. Cinthi picknee better do thing properly, else is sickness and badluck coming in the house.'

'Since ahwe come live in Housing Scheme, funeral come like joke,' Lalo said, reflecting on the many wake-houses and funerals he had attended on the Estate. True. Is everybody involved. Was like everybody funeral. Everything going according to pandit instructions. You keeping wake three nights after the burial. You singing bhajan and talk story til cock crow. Then you doing the seven-day dead wuk, and offer food at graveside. Shree Bhagawan self please with funeral... 'People na know how to keep funeral this time,' Lalo said, his face saddened. He felt he had lost something precious since living in the village.

'Chu chu chu...' Sumintra shook her head, chewing. Big-Bye mooma watched the grass guardedly, not trusting Sumintra who hawked out black tobacco any damn place.

Lalo took out a Capstan tin from his tattered, left-side trousers pocket and began rolling tobacco between his palms. He made a cigarette after plucking a leaf from a book of cigarette papers. Big-Bye mooma watched the operation. She noted how Lalo's fingers trembled. Poor food. Onion and rice, she guessed... Old age showing in Lalo too. But she knew that Lalo's sinews were still strong. It was he who had directed the splitting of the firewood used in the cooking for Big-Bye's wedding, as he had done at many other wedding-houses. Folks consulted him when planning weddings and other ceremonies feeling they couldn't do without his advice.

But what vexed Big-Bye mooma, made her want to skin the small boys in the village, was when she heard how they taunted Lalo. They would rub his head, asking him if he still 'getting stand', call him ole man paapee and hustle to throw his walking stick in the drains at the side of the street.

'They na get respect fo they own mooma who make them,' Big-Bye mooma would tell Sumintra. 'Think they na get respect fo Lalo, eh? If me ever catch them, me skin them behind like fowl. Then they know Lalo fo true.'

She and Sumintra would plan how to trap the little boys. They would loiter on the street-corners baiting them as the boys rummaged in the drains for silverbait fish.

'And ahwe going take out they pants, and rub pepper pon them lolee. They playing big man nuh,' Sumintra would say.

But the little boys would never interfere with Lalo when the two old women were there. They were afraid of Big-Bye mooma and Sumintra and always scooted away from their presence.

'Them lady mouth ain't get eleven o'clock,' they complained. 'Them lady mouth going non-stop. Rememba how they been take out Vishnu pants an rub salt in he beetee cause Vishnu give them hot-mouth. Boy, me na want them rub salt in me beetee, or in me lolee. Is how me going to pee...?'

They wished something terrible would happen to Big-Bye mooma and Sumintra. 'Somebody should throw cow-ich pon them. They shoulda dead wid them eye open. They shoulda get cohcohbeh pon them foot so they can't walk in the road.'

Big-Bye mooma liked it when Lalo visited her. She valued his advice and loved to hear him talk on the *Gita* and the *Ramayana*. She knew too that Lalo liked to be out of his house where he lived with his son and wife and their two children. He had told her it no longer felt like his own home.

She saw how restless Lalo was, as though he was haunted by something. Don't matter how he tried to pass his retirement years in the round of jhandees, wakes and wedding-houses, something seemed to eat him. He talked about feeling an emptiness and she could see it especially at religious occasions; at such times she prayed to Shree Bhagawan to exercise mercy, to release Lalo from the restlessness which gripped him.

As she lay in the hammock, listening to him talking, memories of Lalo would come back. Eh-eh, he was one strong canecutter... he earn more year-end bonus than any of de res'. Dey use to respec' he then. Dey say once people see yuh drinking with Lalo, nobody could tek they eye an' pass you. Was true... But that estate time. Me remember good the story 'bout he an' Souza. This Souza was a very bad, bullyish man. He was estate ranger... suppose to upkeep the logies, but he spend all he time spyin' on we fo' Big Manager, takin bribe an' fixin up tings fo he own self. Eheh, but me fo'get, was not Souza who start this ting but Baichu. He one wicked young chap. He make a nuisance of heself with Lalo unmarried sister. He tell all ahwe that he gone marry she. Lalo bap get vex. No chamaar coming in he high nation chatriya family he tell all de neighbour. Was Lalo who they send to Baichu to warn he to stay away. But the nex' day this Baichu make heself disgusting with Lalo sister again. Lalo in one rage when he hear. He go to Baichu logie to stop this rass-pass. Dey say Baichu come out he logie fighting with he shovel-stick, but Lalo bait he like one stickman, catch he off balance, lift he 'bove he head an' throw he down like one sack a' rice... Was then this Souza come in story. Eh-eh, Baichu give this Souza three-four dollar fo mash up Lalo ass and he agree. But same thing happen to Souza. He try to baton Lalo wid he hakkia, but Lalo bait he, knack he down, kick he up and throw he in de trench. This Souza don't trouble Lalo again. This Souza tink he was power man in de estate til ahwe Lalo mash he up.

Was a time too when Lalo tek on Head Ranger. Eh-eh, dis Head Ranger come down in Nigger-Yard one morning, hunting through dem logies like beast to throw out worker who sick and not in field. Was one sickly chap name Khemraj who have back-pain and paralyse in he feet. This Khemraj resting in he logie taking he food. Head Ranger bawl at he and then baton he cup out he mouth. This Khemraj frighten too bad, but he don't say nothing. Head

Ranger think he stubborn and kick he in he private. Is when Lalo hear this Khemraj call out he wade out he logie an' stand in Head Ranger path. Head Ranger fire one baton at Lalo, but he catch it an' fall pon Head Ranger and cuff he and punch he till he beg fo mercy. Lalo tell he that if he tell Big Manager he gon kill he an' tek bruk-neck. Head Ranger na tell no one, but all ahwe know. Was Khemraj heself who tell me.

This Lalo use to be a terrier, eh-eh; then she watched him sitting there, his body shrunken and his hands trembling, and her memories faded.

EIGHT

One Tuesday morning, two weeks later, Data felt like going to the shop at the head of the street. Since she had started to live with Big-Bye, she had only visited the market once; Big-Bye mooma did the marketing during the midweek days. Data said nothing about this, nor did she complain that Big-Bye never offered to take her out for evening walks. All she knew was that Big-Bye wanted her in the nights. She tolerated this, knowing it was her duty.

But this day, after taking the midday lunch, she couldn't resist the urge to go out. She wanted to make an impression. People in the street still referred to her as 'doolahin', a name which would stay with her until another doolahin came to live in the street. She wanted people to know her by her name.

In the hot, suffocating bedroom she tried on many dresses but they were mostly too long, dropping far below the knee-cap. She stewed her teeth, feeling that the long dresses made her look shapeless and careless of her appearance. She looked at herself in the dressing-table mirror: she *was* shapely, rounded hip, fine waist, plump chest. She admired her nipples which seemed to have become more prominent since her marriage. Good, she told herself and began scrounging among the dresses in the drawer. She picked up one she loved, and had hardly worn. It was a polka-dot polyester, sewed in modern style – low-neck, hipster-bottom, knee-cap length. She decided on this dress. After rubbing powder on her chest and cheeks, she put it on.

When she adjusted the waistline her hips stood out. She was pleased. She smeared a bit of lipstick on her lips, determined to make a good impression.

'Anytime you leave you house to go out, always make one good appearance,' her mother said. 'The more you dress decent an' look clean, the more people respect you.'

Certain now that she looked impressive, Data picked up an empty aerated soft-drink bottle, and walked down the front stairs, her rubber slippers going plop plop.

Big-Bye mooma lay in the hammock, dozing. Data had to inform her where she was going. It was her duty. She called: 'Ma, Ma. Wake up.'

Big-Bye mooma jerked her head as though stung by a marabunta. She lashed her hands wildly about her body, blinking her eyes repeatedly. 'Them marabunta. Me na know what they want with me,' she said angrily, and slumped in the hammock, eyes closed.

Data walked up to her, smiling. 'Ma, is me, I going to buy sweet drink.'

Big-Bye mooma opened her eyes and looked at Data. She blinked, puzzled. She surveyed Data. She blinked again, not believing her eyes.

'What! You going shop? You want street people shame me, and young boy whistle at you, eh. Take out that monkey dress this minute,' she barked.

Data was stunned. Bewildered. The smile dissolved.

'But Ma,' she faltered.

'Ma, me head. Take out that monkey dress this minute,' Big-Bye mooma snapped, eyes reddened now, foam flecking the corners of her lips.

Data hesitated, wondering what to do, her eyes glued on Big-Bye mooma.

'You want shame me. Take out that kiss-me-ass dress this minute,' Big-Bye mooma demanded, pointing her fingers and glaring at Data ferociously. 'Tight dress! Eh-eh?'

Data's nerve broke. She looked around, then bolted upstairs. She slumped onto the bed, crying, burying her head in the mattress.

Big-Bye mooma's hoarse voice echoed from under the house: 'Short dress eh-eh! Is what she want show? Shame and disgrace? That is fo them gal who like cinema and party; and like ride bicycle like man. Not fo me doolahin. Eh-eh, think me going allow that nonesense in front me face... Want people throw dust in me eye?'

Data sobbed. Was it sacrilege for a Hindu girl to be seen wearing a knee-length dress? Most young girls, married or unmarried, wore such dresses. What happen to me? Why Big-Bye mooma against wearing such a dress?

And how she loved that dress. Her mother had liked it too. She knew she had drawn admiring looks when she had worn it and walked the redbrick road in their village. But that was not why she had worn it; it was simply that the dress made her feel good about herself, proud of her good looks and figure.

As her sobs abated, she could hear Big-Bye mooma still firing off in explosions of disgust under the house. She wished herself back in her own village.

Her mother had never complained when she and her sisters wore short dress. 'Is not what you wear,' her mother said, 'Is what in you mind. Some people does wear fancy dress but they mind nasty. Other people could wear old dress, but they mind clean.' And is some people who look at you and they mind clean, and some who mind dirty, Data added to herself. But why me have to wear long dress because it have boys who eyes too fast?

As Data got off the bed and wiped her face, she noted that Big-Bye mooma had stopped her complaining. She changed into another dress, the hemline dropping inches below the knee-cap, and decided to sleep. Some time to come I have to wear that dress, she told herself. She recalled something the seamstress had once said: 'Once you living a decent life, nobody could say you eye black. And never make you mother-in-law control you.'

Suppose Big-Bye mooma want control me? Data asked herself, turning in the bed. She knew Big-Bye mooma had a firm grip on Big-Bye. But that was normal; Big-Bye was her son. She didn't mind that Big-Bye and his mooma had private conversations some evenings in the kitchen, though another daughter-in-law might have felt left-out. She wasn't going to rave or rant as some daughters-in-law were known to do. They were mother and son, and were entitled to some privacy. And she hadn't complained that Big-Bye continued to give his mooma his weekly pay-packet. Nobody could say that since getting married she hadn't been acting the dutiful daughter-in-law. So far she had done nothing which her mother-in-law had any reason to be angry about.

But O Gaad, don't tell me what to wear. I am not the mother of four children. Though Big-Bye is the son, he is a married now, she reasoned. She felt lost, uncertain what to do next and then she drifted into uneasy sleep.

She woke in mid-afternoon, her face puffed with sleep and crying. The village was still drowsing, though healthy winds had started to blow from the Atlantic. She went downstairs to the kitchen, and began preparing to cook the evening meal. She decided to be more mindful of her own wishes from now, telling herself she was no middle-aged woman with four children, that she must able to dress how she felt.

Big-Bye mooma was in the backyard, rummaging among the plants and the fowl-pen. Attracted by the movements in the kitchen, she raised her head and greeted Data, smiling. Data barely acknowledged her, keeping a close interest in the wares she was washing in the sink.

'Doolahin, cook roti and dal,' Big-Bye mooma ordered, then shouted angrily: 'This blasted fowl trying to pick me, eh. Me going show she who is fowl, and who is woman.' She then picked-up a coconut-branch broom lying nearby and began brooming the fowl. The fowl dodged her, cackling;

the chicks scattered, seeking refuge among the plants. 'This kiss-me-ass mother-hen playing hide-an-seek with me, eh. Only Gaad save you life. If you na have chicken, me woulda kill you this Sunday. True. Me woulda bhoonjal you nice,' Big-Bye mooma threatened, chasing the frightened fowl about the yard.

Data blew the chula-fire with the pukni, averaged the heated water, then went for the rice. The fire smoked then blazed, the split redwood crackling. Data coughed, eyes watering. She think me is Big-Bye, nuh. Me own mooma don't tell me how to dress, and why Big-Bye mooma should tell me how to dress? She think me is Paro, nuh!

Paro was Data's left-side neighbour, living in a one bedroom, wooden building. Paro had come to the village two years back when she had been married to a canecutter. She was a simple, quiet-looking girl, plain, with flattened face and small hip.

'Paro modin-law really wukkin she out,' village folks said. 'From marning til night time Paro on she foot. And she modin-law like queen, eh.'

Data knew about Paro. Sometimes she felt sorry for her. Paro did everything in the house: washing, cooking, daubing, milking the mother-in-law's cow and doing the morning puja. She also had to visit the temple with her mother-in-law on Sunday mornings. If Paro's mother-in-law said, 'Sit-down,' Paro sat. Whilst most of the young, married girls dressed to suit themselves and sat together at the village's religious functions, Paro wore long, plain-looking, cheap shamberry dresses and would sit among the older women, listening to every word the pandit said.

'That woman na get feeling fo she own datin-law, eh,' folks said whenever they spotted Paro at a religious ceremony. 'This is not long time. At least them picknee getting education today. And they should plan they own life. And too much house-wuk is the cause why Paro ain't getting picknee. She modin-law ole rass going pay fo she sin...'

Tink me is Paro, huh, Data sucked her teeth, throwing the split-peas in the smaller pot. Wait til me go bed with Big-Bye, wait...

That evening Data observed closely as Big-Bye mooma accosted Big-Bye by the washstand as he came out of the wooden bathroom, and told him something in a lowered tone. Big-Bye nodded absentmindedly, hurrying to change. Data couldn't decipher the words. She was in the kitchen, preparing the evening tea, but she had strong suspicions what Big-Bye mooma was telling him about.

'Big-Bye, you like girl with short dress?' Data asked quietly, eyes on the painted wooden wall, dividing the two bedrooms. They had just made love. Big-Bye felt calm and relaxed.

'Yes Data,' he answered, caressing her breast. He recalled the many evenings when he and his friends had whistled at girls wearing short dresses walking the main street.

'Gosh, look shape,' one of his friends would remark, watching the girls hungrily, wondering how fat their thighs were.

'What about the bottom,' another friend would say, whistling. 'It must be more sweet than sugar plum.'

Big-Bye no less than his friends liked watching girls clad in short dresses, wishing during his sleepless and unmarried nights that his wife would look exactly like one of those girls.

'If me wear short dress one-one time, you going object?' Data asked casually, caressing Big-Bye chest.

'No!' Big-Bye answered, trying to picture Data in a short dress. She would look good, he told himself, imagining the eyes that would be admiring her if she walked the street. He knew she had good shape.

'But you mooma going object when me wear short dress?' Data asked testily.

'You mad or what girl?' Big-Bye replied, slightly flustered. 'You is me wife. And if I want you to wear short dress, me mooma can't say nothing. This is not Estate days.'

At least Big-Bye could think for himself. Fathom certain things. Not so illiterate as some young canecutters, Data told herself. Me know what to do now, she thought, sighing, aware of intermittent raindrops rumbling on the aluminium rooftop. It was getting cold outside.

NINE

On Thursday the following week, it was Janam Astami, Lord Krishna's birthday. Early in the morning Big-Bye mooma began cleaning the yard. She weeded the grass that clustered round the flower-roots, swept the street in front of the house, and cleaned the altar in the eastern section of the yard. Occasionally she glanced at the red-flagged jhandee bamboos, planted near the altar, reminding herself that she had to do a next jhandee. She was in a solemn but joyful mood, bursting out with a Hindi bhajan at every turn she made in the yard.

At midday Sumintra walked in, chewing black tobacco and commenting on the yard's spotlessness. 'Me just clean up meself, gal,' she said, sitting on a bench under the warm bottom-house.

'Today is a special day. Me still thankful to get life in me body,' Big-Bye mooma said, joining Sumintra. Such days gave her life a meaning. They spiced its blandness; though they sharpened the nostalgia for living on the estate where every part of life revolved around the gods and their observance. She believed now that devoting herself to the gods was the only purpose left in her life. To deviate from that path was to find only emptiness, haunting memories, bereft of any glory or pride.

'If you nuh pray and do puja, gal Sumintra,' Big-Bye mooma often said, 'loneliness kill you. Never know Estate life coulda make you turn nothing in you ole age.'

She and Sumintra decided to take offerings of sweetmeat to the temple later in the evening, pray in the Shiv Mandir, then listen to the pandit discourse on the significance of Lord Krishna's birthday to all Hindus.

Data had gotten her orders for the day: clean the house, cook dal, rice and calaloo. No fish and shrimp could be brought in the kitchen; sweetmeats and vermicelli would be prepared later in the afternoon. 'And me going help you,' Big-Bye mooma told her.

Data was used to such days. In her parents' home, too, they were observed in strict accordance with instructions in the holy books. Her mother, too, prayed on such evenings, then visited the temple, Data and her sisters accompanying her. When she sat in the temple listening to the pandit, Data had always been intrigued by the flower-garlanded paintings of the gods around the inner sanctum. They were painted with a garish brightness which made them look lively to Data, whilst their benign smiles and their pastoral settings made her feel that the gods inhabited a world free of sickness, suffering and death. Data longed to visit that world. The pandit's discourse made it sound enchanting.

'But Ma,' Data had asked one evening. 'Why we can't live in them devta world?'

'Because ahwe nuh work out ahwe karma.'

'What is karma?'

'Action. Everybody get a purpose in living. When Shree Bhagawan see that ahwe life is clean, then he going decide to put ahwe in they world,' her mother explained, but hesitantly, as if pondering the mystery of such hopes. 'That is why I always tell you to live a clean life, and respect ole people,' she added.

As she cleaned the bedroom now, Data felt immersed in the sacredness of this day, knowing the spirit of Lord Krishna might be watching her. Living without praying is like bucket without bottom. Is ahwe only consolation in this Estate, she recalled her grandmother saying.

Under the bottom-house Sumintra was telling Big-Bye mooma, 'Me tell me doolahin to press me white dress and orhni. Never mind it ole, me want it look clean.'

'You damn right,' Big-Bye mooma replied, but reflected that whilst she kept her own white dress and orhni clean, if Sumintra only had just two shots of rum in her head, she began jabbering about her dead husband, her loneliness, how backdam wuk had given her nothing, and, all too soon, spittle or driblets of alcohol would soil the white dress she wore. Though Big-Bye mooma warned her, 'Watch you white dress, gal,' Sumintra never cared. 'Why bother, Big-Bye ma? What this life gat to offer? When me take daro me fuget bout meself. This white dress is just false. Is not the dress, is you mind.'

Such words quelled Big-Bye mooma's concern for Sumintra's white dress. Eh-eh, let Sumnintra drink whole night, she would say to herself. When Sumintra dead, is she gat to answer to Shree Bhagawan.

As the afternoon drew to an end, the aroma of sweet-meats cooking in countless kitchens hung over the yards and streets. People began to feel the influence of the day's solemnity; many made resolutions to start living clean lives as the holy books taught.

The evening came with its special brightness. White-dressed women, orhni-clad, were in their front yards offering flower-filled brass plates at their altars. As they placed the flowers and sweetmeats on the altars, they broke into bhajans, feeling purified.

After doing her own puja, Big-Bye mooma walked into the kitchen and said: 'Doolahin, come let me bless you.'

Data obeyed. Big-Bye mooma passed the thari over Data's head seven times, mumbling Hindi words, wishing her health and long life. She did the same to Big-Bye, then walked into her bedroom.

Fifteen minutes later Big-Bye mooma and Sumintra joined other white-dressed women processing to the temple by the Public Road, across the stream. The women carried brass plates filled with flowers and sweetmeats. Electric lights brightened the village though according to the scriptures it was supposed to be a dark night. For older women like Big-Bye mooma and Sumintra this was another sign of how much tradition they had lost since the estate days.

Big-Bye papa went to the temple later, asking his perennial question: 'What difference it make if me going mandir or not? Still want to know the purpose in me life.' Try as he might, Big-bye papa could never feel that he had arrived at any clear or definite idea of what his life should mean. All he could do was to submit himself to what each day brought.

Big-Bye and Data retired to bed knowing love-making was taboo for the night.

One midday, after eating lunch, Data decided to visit the cakeshop. This time she would defy Big-Bye mooma if she objected to how she dressed. She wore a tight-fitting pants and knitted blouse which she had brought along with her other clothes when she had come with Big-Bye on the second Sunday. She knew Big-Bye wouldn't mind.

'Me like when you dress fancy, Data,' he had told her three nights before. 'At least people going say me get one nice wife.'

'But if you mooma nuh like it,' Data had said, testing him. She didn't *want* to offend Big-Bye mooma. She hoped that if she showed her due respect and loyalty, the relationship between them would remain untarnished.

'Is not me mooma gat to like how you dress,' Big-Bye said. 'Is me gat to like it... And you want me friend them tell me, me wife dressing like old woman?'

Data pondered these words as she looked how the pants and blouse fitted, how the pants fitted tightly around the hip. She attributed this development to marriage. 'When you start take the thing regular you hip does get big,' Jasmine had said one morning, about a year ago. They had been in Data's mother's bedroom, trying on each other's dresses.

'But how you know?' Data asked curiously, aware that she was treading on sinful ground.

Chu chu chu... Jasmine shook her head as if pitying Data's ignorance. 'When a woman getting baby you nuh see the hip does first get big.'

'Is true girl,' Data answered, blaming her stupidity.

She smiled now as she adjusted the pants around the hip, wondering if she was pregnant. Can't be, she told herself. Is only six weeks me get married. And only last month me see me courses.

Then she dabbed powder on her face and slapped a little lipstick on her lips. Hadn't Big-Bye said she must look nice whenever she came out of the house?

Pleased with her looks, she picked up an empty aerated-drink bottle from the kitchen and entered the bottom-house. Big-Bye mooma slept in the hammock, her snores punctuated by the whistling sound of mucus shifting in her chest.

As she watched Big-Bye mooma Data could not decide what to do. To tell her or not? Virtue required that she inform Big-Bye mooma that she was going out of the house. To do otherwise was to invite calumny. Only God knew what she would think, what she would tell Big-Bye. Leaving the house without telling anyone? Data shuddered, unable to predict the consequences.

'Ma, Ma! Wake up,' she bent and shook Big-Bye mooma by the shoulders.

Eh-eh, Big-Bye mooma grunted, blinking her eyes in annoyance. Then she raised-up, startled, believing a jumbie had materialised in front of her.

'Eh-eh, is you, doolahin?' Big-Bye mooma said, regaining her composure, sitting upright in the hammock. 'But is what me seeing?' she blurted, eyeing Data from head to foot. She couldn't believe her eyes. Me own doolahin, she told herself. Look me shame.

'You playing man, eh? And you want burn down Garge-town with you lip? Look, take out this blasted man clothes this minute before me mad blood raise,' she ordered, face contorted in passion.

Data flinched as though hit by a thunderbolt, slow paralysis invading her body.

'You is fullah woman fo wear pants, eh? Gaad make you one woman, not man,' Big-Bye mooma remarked. 'Is not because we live in high house, get well-pipe in we yard, radio in we house, newspaper at we gate, mean woman going turn man. Eh-eh.'

'But Ma, Big-Bye say is okay to wear pants,' Data tried to assure her, eyes pleading. Pants and blow is not blasphemy against the Hindu religion. Data knew of many respectable Hindu girls who wore pants and blow, some living in this village. But however respectable the girl, it made no differ-ence to the remarks Big-Bye mooma threw at them.

'Eh-eh, is women like them does give the Hindu reli-gion bad name. If them been want wear pants them shoulda turn fullah woman and black woman. Eat pork and beef and go party.'

Data would turn a deaf ear to such remarks, barely glancing at the girls, fearing to provoke further Big-Bye mooma's anger.

Chu chu chu... Big-Bye mooma would pout her lips, then smack her tongue as if she had eaten sour mango. 'Is women like them who does take man from they husband-head, doolahin,' she would say, wanting to retch. 'But look what the Hindu religion coming to? Me been wonder to know if them picknee papa don't feel shame today when them see them own own picknee, gal picknee in pants. Is true thing. The more you live is the more you seeing...'

Those remarks echoed in Data's ears. But now she was determined to defy. 'But Ma, I just going to the shop and come back.'

'Doolahin,' Big-Bye mooma screamed. 'Take out this

gymnastic clothes now now. Me nuh want shame fall in me door.'

Chuuuuu... Data pouted her lips, stamped her feet defiantly, and walked out of the yard.

'Are baap ray! Look what happening to me life,' Big-Bye mooma screamed again, calling in the direction of Sumintra's house. 'Hey Sumintra, come see what happening. Sumintra. O Shree Bhagawan!' Big-Bye mooma began beating her chest, foam gathering at the corners of her lips, eyes blazing.

'Mai gone out, Big-Bye mooma,' Sumintra's daughter-in-law shouted through the kitchen window, curious to know what had happened.

'Is arite, doolahin,' Big-Bye mooma answered, walking under the house, chattering. 'Wait til me Big-Bye come, wait. Look this disgrace in me ole age. Pants and shirt! Eh-eh!'

Data was careful not to look to see if there were any eyes peering at her as she entered the shop, though inwardly she sensed she had made an impression. She felt nice, though still shaken by Big-Bye mooma's attitude. The woman believe me make four picknee aready. Modin-law should not dictate you life. This is not long time. Such thoughts rioted in Data's mind until she arrived back in the yard.

'You going out you bounds nuh,' Big-Bye mooma said when Data returned. She pointed her fingers at her. Data ignored her and walked straight into the kitchen.

'Doolahin!' Big-Bye mooma shouted, following Data. Data halted, staring at Big-Bye mooma.

'You watching at me like when cow break rope,' Big-Bye mooma accused, facing Data.

Data, cowed, inched away. She was frightened that Big-Bye mooma might hit her. She had heard of many quarrels between mothers and daughters-in-law which had ended in blows. Some mothers-in-law even believed they had a right to beat their daughters-in-law. And the mother-in-law always gained the sympathy of the household and the neighbours.

Data didn't want anything like that to happen. That would be to her shame. She had just got married. What would people say? 'Oh that Data. Eh-eh, girl, she is something. She warrish and she giving she modin-law hot-mouth.'

'When you see so, she must be done take man before she married. And because the modin-law not finding blood in she sheet the second Sunday night, she making story to frighten the modin-law.' Data dreaded the thought of such remarks being thrown at her. How would she walk the road? Her head hung in shame?

She moved to turn away, to end the confrontation, but Big-Bye mooma, sweating in the heat, demanded her attention.

'If you been know you like short dress and pants, you shoulda tell me when me been come ask home fo you,' Big-Bye mooma said. She feared for her son and for herself and for the altar. 'It show like me really gat to do one jhandee.'

Data went into the kitchen. She wondered what Big-Bye mooma was trying to say, why wearing pants seemed so threatening to her. Then she went upstairs, changed and lay on the bed, wondering what she would tell Big-Bye when he came home.

Downstairs, Big-Bye mooma grumbled to herself. Is the pandit duty to warn parents how to control them picknee dressing. Soontime them picknee going walk naked in the street, and they call it style. Today-eddication and Christain bottom-house church corrupting the Hindu religion. True. Me really gat to talk with pandit.

Big-Bye mooma's words echoed upstairs as Data willed herself to sleep, trying to forget. When she woke some time after three, Big-Bye mooma was still in the back garden, venting her feelings on the fowls and complaining of the afternoon heat. She fanned herself, panting for breath. She felt her life's purpose was being defeated by Data's intrusion. She vowed to curb it.

Hearing footsteps in the kitchen, she knew Data had

come down to prepare the evening meal. 'Cook roti,' she shouted, her tone menacing.

'Yes Mai,' Data answered timidly.

'Nuh mai me. Mai Big-Bye when he come home,' Big-Bye mooma added in mocking irritation. The woman come like setting-fowl, Data told herself and resumed her chores.

Big-Bye mooma found various pretexts for staying in the garden, shuttling between the chicken pen and the plants; and as soon as Big-Bye arrived from the backdam around six, she rushed out of the backyard, and shouted: 'Big-Bye, Big-Bye, come!'

Though Big-Bye sensed the urgency in her tone, he disappeared under the house, glancing at Data in the kitchen, to get ready for a bath. His face was darkened with smears of cane-ash. He felt tired. Today's canecutting was tough. Sorry I never learn tailoring, he admitted to himself.

'Big-Bye, this woman want bring shame and disgrace to me,' Big-Bye mooma said, pointing in the kitchen at Data. She was incensed. Her body trembled slightly.

Big-Bye looked bewildered. He wanted to know what his mooma meant. His eyes roved between Data and his mooma. He felt uneasy.

'She wear pants and shirt this midday and go shop,' Big-Bye mooma complained, watching Data accusingly.

'Oh!' Big-Bye sighed, showing no interest. He turned towards the bathroom.

Big-Bye mooma waited. She was enraged. Tikkay this woman controlling me son, she thought, alarmed. 'But is shame and disgrace to we religion,' she shouted.

To argue was to start a quarrel, Big-Bye reasoned, knowing the depth of his mooma's temper. To him, Data had done nothing wrong, but he had to give his mooma some satisfaction.

'Me going talk to she,' Big-Bye said, masking his irritation with his mother and glaring at Data in the kitchen.

Data was stunned. What? she asked herself. Like Big-Bye on he mooma side. Wait til me go bed tonight.

'Right, Big-Bye, put she in she place,' Big-Bye mooma said, feeling a release. 'She want bring shame and disgrace to we religion,' she added, heading for the garden. 'And is them pundit fault, too. They preaching politics in mandir...'

TEN

Twice now before retiring to bed that night Big-Bye mooma had complained, 'Ow Gaad, like me head bursting.' She held her forehead and groaned as if she was dying. She lay in the hammock. Data rushed out of the kitchen in alarm. 'What happen Mai? What happen?' she asked, bending low in front of her.

'Ow me head, like it going to burst,' Big-Bye mooma repeated, clutching her forehead. Is *you* cause this kiss-me-ass headache, she thought, watching Data with slanted eyes.

Big-Bye papa brought Limocal from upstairs and began massaging his wife's forehead with it. He listened to the crickets and beetles noising in the yard. Darkness crawled in, repelled only slightly by a low-wattage bulb in the bottom-house.

'Me tell you don't worry so much, woman,' he said quietly, sitting near his wife. He lit a Lighthouse cigarette. 'You too ole fo worry,' he added, exhaling smoke, his eyes roving the houses, each lit by their dim electric bulbs, all constructed from loans from the Sugar Labour Welfare Fund Committee, all occupied by sugar workers who had lived most of their lives on the estate. Working like jackass all these years, and is only this we gat to show? he asked himself, moving his eyes in a sweeping gesture. Gaad! he sighed. The urge to escape, to drown in alcohol gripped him. Why me couldn't born somewhere else, he added, cursing his fate. 'Or tun bird.'

Data left. He turned to Big-Bye mooma, bitterness

curling his cigarette-stained lips. 'Why you nuh relax, eh? You headache going stop,' he said in a mocking tone.

'Heh, is everything me going look after?' Her voice rang in irritation as she adjusted herself in the hammock.

'Arite, woman, arite,' Big-Bye papa said tiredly, with utter disgust for life. 'You headache come from ole age and worry,' he added, lighting another cigarette.

Big-Bye mooma couldn't tell him that Data was the real cause of her headache. The pants and the blow. And the damn fool Big-Bye didn't tell she anything about it. Big-Bye just change and gone road-top. He nuh care one ass what Data doing. Me going show him who is the mooma. Wait and see...

Three quarters of an hour later, Big-Bye mooma had another attack. This time Big-Bye was in the kitchen having his evening tea, thinking about a discussion that had gone on at the Party meeting. 'If we ain't mobilize we self, comrades, we could never kick out the white people and nationalise Bookers and Demba,' the Party spokesman had said. 'The more you educate yourself is better for the cause. Is time we run we own affairs.'

Blah, Big-Bye had mocked. Since the Party in power, things still the same. Me still have to work hard in canefield. What difference it make?

He decided to boycott future Party meetings until something concrete was done by the Party's union to improve working conditions in the canefields. These thoughts were interrupted by his mooma's groan. He dashed out of the kitchen, rushing to her hammock asking, 'What happen, Mai?' heart beating in panic.

'Just me head, Big-Bye, just me head...' she moaned.

Big-Bye felt helpless. He cared for his mooma deeply, despite her sometimes irritating ways. But she was his mooma. 'Never turn your back against you old parents. You going punish,' folks said. He shouted: 'Data. Come see Mai.'

Data was taking her evening bath, a habit she had culti-
vated since growing up. She loved to keep herself clean.
'Girl when you bathe you does smell nice,' Big-Bye had told
her one night.

'You nuh see me bathing,' she shouted.

'But Mai head hurting,' Big-Bye added in desperation,
eyes darting between the bathroom and his mooma.

'Ow beta, Big-Bye!' his mooma groaned, rubbing her
forehead. 'Nobody nuh care fo me,' she said, her eyes cast
down, as though she needed a long rest.

While she was massaging Big-Bye mooma's head with
the Limocol, Data suspected that her headache was not as
serious as she claimed. Is something in the woman mind,
she decided, recalling past instances when her own mother
experienced similar headaches because she was worrying
over something.

Data tried to soothe Big-Bye mooma with as much
tenderness as she could muster. At last Big-Bye mooma felt
wanted. After all Data is a good doolahin, she told herself,
but me can't understand this dressing. And me gat to stop it.

Gradually her headache eased.

In bed that night Data felt agitated. She was not sure
whether Big-Bye had liked her to dress in that manner or
not. This evening's incident gave her cause for thought.
'Big-Bye, you like when me dressing with pants and shirt?'
she whispered, her tone serious.

'Yes girl,' he replied, hugging Data.

She shied away. 'But is why you mooma nuh like when
me dress?' she asked quietly, aware that Big-Bye mooma, in
the next bedroom, was probably not asleep. She could hear
her turning restlessly in her bed, sighing, making muffled
groans. Big-Bye papa snored intermittently.

'You must tell you mooma that is *you* who does tell me to
dress,' she urged. 'Yes yes,' he answered, caressing Data's
thighs. He knew he couldn't tell his mooma what Data
asked of him. He was afraid. His mooma would say: 'You

picking up fo you wife, nuh. You not care what people say. You nuh care if them young boy whistle at you wife. Eh-eh, look the shame!'

Big-Bye feared the confrontation with his mooma but liked it when Data looked fancy. Yes! the boys would say, 'Never mind Big-Bye cutting cane but he get choice. You must see he wife when she dress up. She is no stupid woman. She is a modern woman.' Big-Bye would relish such remarks, would feel proud walking in the streets. I gat to convince me mooma that this is not Estate time, he told himself, starting to mount Data.

Big-Bye mooma could not sleep. She was tempted to wake up Big-Bye papa but thought better of it. Me never know what eating that man... and up to now me son nuh tell doolahin bout the pants and blow she wear today. But is what getting into Big-Bye head since he get wife, eh? Me dead-sure doolahin put nasty thing in he food. Have to tell Sumintra.'

But no matter how hard she strained her eardrums she couldn't pick up a word of what Big-Bye and Data were saying in their bedroom. Is only whispering... whispering. And the bed creaking. Gaad, like that woman want dry me son back, she sighed, tasting bitter saliva in her mouth. She wanted to call out to them to stop. She turned heavily and coughed. Strong Atlantic winds, blowing in gusts, pounded the roof-top, rustling leaves and flowers.

Like rain going to fall, Big-Bye mooma thought. Me can't understand. Me son did always pick up fo me. She recalled the many times Big-Bye had shouted at his papa. 'You better don't insult Mai,' he would say, watching his papa squarely.

Such incidents occurred rarely now but used to happen whenever Big-Bye papa, already drunk, demanded more money to buy high wine. She would refuse and he would explode: 'If you nuh want give me money, ask Shree Bhagawan to stop me from drinking...'

'Ask Shree Bhagawan youself, you damn shaitan,' she

would fire back viciously. 'Me tell you rum have evil spirit inside.'

'Look woman, give me the money,' he would say, advancing, his eyes threatening.

Big-Bye mooma would scream, believing he wanted to hit her.

The scream usually attracted Big-Bye. Big-Bye papa would grin and walk away, watching at Big-Bye. 'The day you pit you hand pon me, me going show you who is big man,' he would threaten, pointing his fingers at his son. 'Keep that in the canefield and fo you friends.'

But Big-Bye knew he couldn't hit his papa. 'Never raise you hand at you parents, don't matter how they wrong,' folks said. 'If you parents' eye-water catch you, you never righted til you dead...'

When Big-Bye papa sobered up, the quarrel between father and son was forgotten, but he dreaded his wife's tongue. She would rail at him, her every word biting, vicious like a snake.

Is what really come over this Big-Bye, she asked herself again. Suppose doolahin doing something to him? Can't trust nowadays young gal. They know how to control man. Put 'thing' in they husband food. Quick time they going obeah man and pandit. Eh-eh, suppose doolahin doing thing to Big-Bye and me son get mad? Her thoughts strayed to Rusty.

Rusty had been a quiet, decent Hindu boy working in the Estate Irrigation Gang. Dutiful towards his parents. He hardly drank or smoked. Three months after Rusty got married he started nagging and quarrelling with his mother. Demanded to live his own life. Moved out his parents' home with his wife. Hit his father. Supported his wife a hundred percent. Cast a blind eye on his wife's indulgences: fancy dresses, cinema-going, black-pudding and beef-eating...

A year later Rusty suffered a nervous breakdown. He was sent to the Georgetown Hospital's Observation Ward.

'She used to put menstruation blood in Rusty curry,' folks said. 'She used to run at all them obeah man fo get Rusty under she control,' others alleged, shaking their heads in pity. 'And Rusty was such a good boy.'

'Rusty wife is not woman. Rusty wife is snake,' some women remarked. 'Woman like them only respect cut-rass. Rusty was too easy...'

O Gaad, me nuh want that to happen to Big-Bye, his mooma sighed fearfully. Nowadays young girl know too much. Never mind Big-Bye is first man fo doolahin, still me can't trust. Me gat to see Sumintra and Lalo tomorrow, she decided, wishing the night would pass quickly.

Winds raged outside, howling, echoing. A blackbird hooted as it flew above the house. O Gaad, me know something bad going happen. Big-Bye mooma shuddered, covering her head. Me hope nobody dead in the street. She tossed and turned for some time longer before she slept. Big-Bye and Data were already sleeping.

It was overcast the next morning. Most folks wished that rain would fall. They thought of the plants and fruit trees struggling to grow in the backyards, the half-dried drains and stunted grasses. But by the time Sumintra and Lalo came the sun was beginning to shine and people were once again lamenting the fate of their plants. But is Gaad work, some had shrugged. Can't fight against fate.

Data couldn't hear what the three old people were talking about as she cleaned the kitchen, and to enter the bottom-house, pretending to sweep it, would be unmannerly. But she noted their conspiratorial attitudes, their lowered voices. She guessed Big-Bye mooma and Sumintra were talking about somebody, and Lalo was agreeing with every word being said.

'Me nuh believe doolahin stay so,' Sumintra whispered, watching the kitchen. 'This time young gal like dress, Big-Bye mooma,' she added, rolling black tobacco in her palms.

'Which young gal nuh like look nice? Look me doolahin. Think me could tell she how to dress? Once the husband like it, modin-law nuh get voice,' Sumintra explained.

But Big-Bye mooma had never respected Sumintra's daughter-in-law. To Big-Bye mooma, Sumintra's daughter-in-law was not a devout Hindu wife. She get fullahman ways, dressing how she damn well please. Laughing ke ke ke like one blackguarded woman, eating pig-foot cook-up. And she mouth hot like fire. And this Sumintra apologising fo she daughter-in-law. Eh-eh, just because she daughter-in-law buying a half bottle rum fo Sumintra every Saturday afternoon. This Sumintra is the same. True...

'But me can't take trust, Sumintra,' Big-Bye mooma whispered, eyes darting in the kitchen.

'Then you must dish out Big-Bye food if you frighten,' Sumintra advised. 'Is not true, Lalo?'

Lalo nodded noncommittally. He weighed the situation and said in a placatory way: 'Not'ing to frighten, Big-Bye mooma. High house an eddication put different sense in young gal head. Tink in Estate lil boy coulda mock me?' Lalo sighed wearily. He never believed he would have seen young men drinking rum in company with their papas, man to man. This could never happen in Estate.

Her friends' assurance that Data wouldn't try to put 'thing' in Big-Bye food, revived Big-Bye mooma. Her eyes brightened. 'Doolahin,' she turned and shouted sweetly. 'Make some coconut choka. Me mouth feel to eat coconut choka with bird pepper and garlic inside.'

Lalo's and Sumintra's mouths watered, hoping it would not be too long before Data finished preparing it.

ELEVEN

As the weeks turned into months, a kind of truce existed between Big-Bye mooma and Data. They greeted each other pleasantly and helped each other with the domestic chores. There were matters on which they saw eye to eye. Big-Bye mooma always insisted that the front yard be kept clean.

'The more clean the place,' she said, 'is better fo the devtas. They would stay more long in the yard and bless the place.'

Data agreed. Folk said: 'Devtas don't come in nasty people place. And is why you think some people can't see they way in life? Cause they place nasty, and it cause them to suffer blight.'

Data was by now wholly familiar with the daily routine. She knew what to do, what to cook that pleased. If she didn't think too much about it she could feel quite at home in this household. But in her moments of relaxation her thoughts rebelled. She knew what she wanted for herself and Big-Bye, but how to get it? She knew he would own the house when his parents died. But that wasn't enough. It was now she wanted to escape from the drudgery of everyday boredom; to find something useful; not to be tied by many children in years to come; not to be living under Big-Bye mooma's iron hand.

But where to begin? Big-Bye mooma still ran the household, dictated all affairs, and received Big-Bye's pay packet as well as his papa's. Data knew she was still powerless to challenge the custom established between mother and son since the first Friday afternoon when, as a sixteen year old, after his first week of work in the mule gang, he had given his mooma his pay packet.

With the passing of each night Big-Bye felt himself drawn closer to Data. He liked to be seen walking in the street with her. She sensed his growing attachment, but she never consciously turned it to her own advantage. Never tried to embarrass him or chide his still sometimes childish attitudes. She made sure the relationship between Big-Bye and his mooma ran smoothly, and always praised Big-Bye mooma in his presence. Big-Bye knew his mooma didn't always warrant such praise but he couldn't tell Data. Once his Mooma and Data understood each other, all was well and good for him.

One midday as Big-Bye mooma lay asleep in the hammock, Sumintra's daughter-in-law, Chan, walked over. The village slept, as though everything existed in a vacuum of silence, a pause, only the cocks tolling the afternoon hours, a quiet wind rippling leaves and flowers.

'Eh girl, since you married you never come over by me,' Chan called, smiling warmly. She was a round-faced woman in her late twenties with full body and large hips.

Data, sat on a wooden bench in the kitchen sifting rice. Chan braced herself on the wall by the kitchen door, still smiling.

'You know how me modin-law stay,' Data said in a lowered voice, craning her neck to make sure Big-Bye mooma was still sleeping.

'Chuu,' Chan pouted her lips in annoyance. 'Look, you gat you life fo live, eh?'

'I know, but I just married,' Data said as though struggling to find the right words.

'How long you think you going live under you modin-law petticoat like Big-Bye?' Chan continued, her tone sarcastic.

Data shrugged her shoulders, but she knew Chan asked the very question which ate into her during the daytime hours of feigned sleep. When an answer couldn't be found, Data put aside the question, and resumed her customary role of duty and obedience. She wanted to make more of her life her own, but could not see how to do it without creating discord in the household, disrupting its smooth-running ways. It was too early.

'Girl, if you nuh try to find you own way, help youself and know what in store fo you future, you going get four-five picknee quick time,' Chan said, shaking her head in pity.

Chan talking sense, Data told herself. She recalled Big-Bye mooma's words: 'You see that Chan. Eh-eh, she is a good thing with she self. When she get passion she giving Sumintra word fo word. Chaach, she shoulda scrub she tongue with blacksage. That is respect for modin-law? She want a fine cut-ass. She think she is man...'

'And leh me tell you one thing, girl,' Chan tried to assume a matronly tone, 'if you nuh talk fo you right, them modin-law ride you like jackass. Them fail to realise this is not Estate days. And you nuh gat to wear orhni and cover you face when you talking to you father-in-law. And ahwe woman not only gat to make picknee and run the house. We have to plan with we husband...'

'Is true,' Data heard herself whisper. And the phrase came back: Where to begin?

'Must come over to gaff one-one time, girl,' Chan invited after enquiring about affairs in Data's village.

Throughout the week Data's mind was in turmoil. Every time she saw Chan through the kitchen window, the words kept hitting her like constant drips of water on sandstone. Is truth Chan talking, she admitted to herself. What a fool I am... married for over three month and don't know how much money in me husband pay packet. Don't know how much money to run the house each week. Nobody consult me about affairs in the house, and is Big-Bye mooma buying everything, and she giving me some money each Saturday like me still one child. This is not much more than a slave. She decided she would visit her mother the coming Sunday morning.

Big-Bye went with her, carrying his mooma's blessings. 'And tell you modin-law me send howdy, you hear Big-Bye?' his mooma reminded him by the front gate. 'And don't stay too late,' she added.

Data's mother welcomed Data and Big-Bye warmly, her smile broad and inviting.

'Eh-eh, like married life greeing with you,' her two sisters teased, eyes surveying Data like seamstresses trying out the fit of a new dress.

Data blushed. Big-Bye felt proud. At least they can't say Data punishing, he told himself. He found himself a seat in the house and began cracking jokes with the sisters, his tone easy and familiar.

The sisters noted with a tinge of envy that Data's hip looked bigger, her bust fuller, and wondered if she was pregnant. But it was not proper to ask her that unless they themselves were married.

Data's mother beamed happily. In her excited mood she ordered the sisters to get a beer for Big-Bye, then penned a fowl to be slaughtered. The midday meal would be dal, rice and bhoonjal chicken.

Big-Bye tried to be his natural self, as though he had visited this home many times before. He walked about, whistled, and chatted with Data's mother about trivial things going on in the village.

'Data pa gone to look after them cow. Me going send to call he,' Data's mother said, anxious to hear how Data was getting on in Big-Bye mooma's home.

'Wait til you get one picknee. Things going change,' her mother said in the big bedroom. She sat beside Data on the bed listening to her story. She tried to understand how Data felt. As a newly married woman she herself had experienced much worse. She remembered in her days that to address your father-in-law without wearing an ornhi was to show utter disrespect; to raise your voice in your mother-in-law's presence was mutiny; you would be called a blackguarded woman, a prostitute. It had been hard, but there had seemed no other way.

But it was not so now, the mother acknowledged. Young people getting more wise. Yet they should strive to upkeep their Hindu religion. Is married life. True. You could only advise them.

'Some modin-law like that you know,' Data's mother cajoled, cupping Data's chin.

Data tried to understand.

'And they want make sure they daughter-in-law good. That she could make picknee,' her mother continued in a soft voice, wondering if Data was pregnant. 'None modin-law nuh want barren daughter-in-law in they house. You know that is shame and disgrace. And you know how much curse it could bring in they house? And don't talk bout the cat-pat.'

'You right, Ma,' Data agreed, hoping she was not barren. She knew of the curses heaped on barren women and the daily tantrums that went on between mothers-in-law and daughters-in-law in such situations. She knew of occasions when the warring factions had used coconut branch brooms on each other until someone made peace between them.

'Them is real witch,' folk remarked of barren women. They were churiles and ol higues. Pregnant women avoided barren women's company, fearing that a barren woman's eyes could harm their babies, deforming them at the hour of delivery.

Data listened to her mother, and promised to bide her time with her mother-in-law until a more understanding relationship was established between them.

No use fighting against me fate, Data told herself, though telling herself this did nothing to lessen what she felt. There was something else she wanted to know, but she felt abashed to ask her mother how she could tell whether she was pregnant or not. She hadn't seen her last month's period and past talk with friends hinted that when a married woman missed her monthly, it somehow meant she was pregnant. She would have to clear up the matter with Chan.

The next day, Monday, about midday, Data walked over to Chan's place when she knew Big-Bye mooma was sleeping in the hammock. Chan was alone; her two children had gone to school and Sumintra was in the back garden moulding the pepper plants.

'Could be you getting baby, girl,' Chan said, breaking into a smile.

Anxiety showed in Data's face. Even with Chan she felt uncomfortable explaining the matter. Chan wasn't certain though. 'Could be that you period delay,' she added. 'Must try drink ginger tea with black pepper inside, just to make sure. And you know what?' Chan continued, lowering her voice conspiratorially, 'Every time you and Big-Bye do the thing, don't get up sametime, else the spence going run down. And you wouldn't get catch.'

'Eh. Is so?' Data shrugged her shoulders, staring in bewilderment. 'Me never hear about this one,' she admitted. 'What I hear is that if the husband and wife break together, the wife bound to be pregnant.'

'Then another thing,' Chan added, 'You and Big-Bye must do the thing when full moon up. The Moon gat something to do with pregnancy old people say, and with woman period...'

'Girl Chan, me never know all this,' Data confessed.

'Chan know plenty things. If you nuh get you period this month, mean that you getting babby,' Chan teased. 'But must try the ginger tea to make sure.'

Data decided she must watch more carefully for changes in her body. After every lunch time she looked at herself in the bedroom mirror. Then, after taking her bath, she would note whether there was any swelling in the breast, especially the nipples. She cupped them and squeezed, trying to extract milk. She knew milk meant pregnancy. She had been startled when a thin, rancid-smelling, whitish liquid oozed out, but not looking much like milk. Data couldn't tell whether this liquid was associated with pregnancy or not. She would have to ask Chan. Big-Bye was a fool. He wouldn't know. Now she noticed the curve in her hip, and a slight rounding of her inner thigh. Still she couldn't decide whether these were signs of pregnancy, though, at the back of her mind, she suspected she *was* pregnant.

She imagined herself in a pregnancy dress and shuddered. Think me still too young to make children, but if is God's wish, me can't do anything about it. She had seen some young married women's beauty tarnished after bearing too many children, their bodies looking flabby and old before their time.

But the seamstress had said, 'Don't matter how much picknee you get, always care youself. The moment you husband lose interest in you looks: careful! He might go to other woman. And you know this time young gal is no fun. Them lil eddication make them wise. And them nuh care about ahwe culture. Beside, when you get too much picknee, you patacake come big and ugly. And man nuh like that at all. So better take me advice serious, Data.'

She damn well right, Data admitted. The seamstress always kept herself smart and clean. It was hard to guess her age for she still had a young girl's body and the village youths talked admiringly of it. But she was also an ardent temple goer. Since knowing her, Data had never heard anybody badmouth her character. Her name was never called with any man. She is a woman to talk about, Data concluded, vowing to pattern her lifestyle on the seamstress's.

But Data's intention of biding her time with her mother-in-law did not last long. It was a Saturday evening. Big-Bye had already bathed and changed, telling Data, 'I going by the roadside, girl,' and left. Big-Bye papa as usual was in the back garden tending the plants, looking forward to the quarter bottle of rum he would be drinking later in the evening after his dal-purri and fish curry. As he communed with the plants he concluded: 'Me lil shot is me only consolation. What more life gat to offer?'

Data had changed and was combing her hair when Big-Bye mooma walked upstairs, a big smile on her face. She placed a brown paper parcel on the table and said affably, 'Me buy one nice dress material fo you, doolahin.'

Data looked pleased. She stopped combing her hair, held the parcel on the table, and began unwrapping it carefully, with respect.

Big-Bye mooma continued to smile. 'See how me like you,' she added, waiting to be complimented.

The moment Data's eyes dropped on the dress-material she looked crestfallen, her saliva turned sour. Impulsively she blurted out: 'This three fo dalla shamberry you want me wear, eh?'

Big-Bye mooma looked startled. Her smile vanished. 'Is good cloth, doolahin. Tink me nuh know to buy?'

'Good cloth fo you,' Data heard herself saying, dashing the cloth on the table as if it were a piece of rag.

Big-Bye mooma felt insulted. Her eyes turned ferocious, challenging. 'You tink you is some queen, eh?' she shouted. 'Or you body get gold. What wrong with this shamberry?'

Data's passion was unleashed. She looked up, anger in her eyes. 'Make petticoat fo youself,' she shouted and headed for the downstairs.

Big-Bye mooma felt crushed, cheapened. This wretch going too far, she told herself and followed Data. 'Like you want bring blight in me house, or you like show you behind in the street? Is only pants and short dress you want, nuh?' she said.

Data slumped in the hammock, feeling tired. I ain't know

this woman is who, she told herself, wishing she had never married into this house.

Data's silence infuriated Big-Bye mooma. Can't take no blasted eye-pass from no kiss-me-ass datin-law. She anchored herself in front of Data, pointing her finger at her. 'I going make Big-Bye give you one fine cut-ass, you wretch you...'

'Who is a wretch like you,' Data fired, her tongue unable to control the words.

'Who you calling wretch, who you calling wretch?' Big-Bye mooma shouted, intent on choking Data. She fell on her, fingers aimed at Data's throat. Data slipped out the hammock but Big-Bye mooma was quick. She clutched at Data's long hair and pulled. Data staggered and screamed.

Big-Bye papa heard the quarrel. He dashed from the backyard, his heart in panic. 'O Bhagawan!' he shouted and leapt at Big-Bye mooma. 'You want kill doolahin, eh?' He caught Big-Bye mooma's fingers and loosened them from Data's hair. 'You mad or what woman?' When Data was free he motioned her to go upstairs.

Data ran, crying.

'Is what you loose me fo, man? Me woulda teach she good sense,' Big-Bye mooma complained, fire still burning in her eyes. 'Give she one inch and she want one foot,' she quarrelled. 'But me going make Big-Bye cut-ass she behind. Tink she is queen. She nuh want wear three yaad fo dalla cloth. She behind must be get gold...' Then Big-Bye mooma burst into tears. 'Is you cause it, is you who tell me to go see doolahin. Is you make me choose she fo Big-Bye wife. She want eye-pass me in me own house. Is only janjhat, janjhat...'

TWELVE

An hour later, as soon as Big-Bye entered the yard, his mooma ran up to him screaming and shouting, 'You wife call me wretch. And pon top she want kill me.'

Big-Bye was stupefied. 'What?'

Tears streamed down his mooma's face, running in her nose, muffling her voice, making the words come out in sputtering fits and starts. 'You wife call me wretch. And she want kill me.'

Hurt and humiliation clouded Big-Bye's face. 'I going deal with she,' he snapped, and strode into the bottom-house, looking for Data.

His mooma followed, complaining: 'Tink me is some plaything fo any kiss-me-ass doolahin push she finger in me face...'

Data was in the kitchen, telling herself how stupidly she had acted. She was angry with herself for losing her temper, she had never wanted to breed ill-feeling between Big-Bye mooma and herself. When people heard they would blame her, saying what a warrish daughter-in-law she was. She would have to walk the street with her head hung in shame. Folks might say mockingly: 'Is what happen with she Hindu culture?'

She would take care not to do that again. But why had she been so carried away? What had so provoked her? Which was to blame. The shamberry or Big-Bye mooma?

'Data! is why you curse me mooma?' Big-Bye shouted, advancing at her, tight-fisted in passion.

Data shuddered, fingers trembling, eyes filled with fright. She backed away, stuttering: 'Is she first start it... start it...'

BLAI

Big-Bye's right palm connected with her left cheek. The slap was unexpected. Data staggered, stunned, her vision blurred.

'Tell me, tell me,' he insisted, rage in his eyes.

'Good fo she. She mouth hot like pepper,' Big-Bye mooma barked, fingers pointing at Data.

Big-Bye attempted another slap but Data was quick. She dodged, baiting him, then dashed upstairs, using the inner house steps.

Big-Bye mooma flung herself on her son and gripped his waist, pulling him back. 'O Gaad beta! Me nuh want you get charge fo murder,' she begged, dragging Big-Bye towards the bottom-house. He didn't resist. Data's cries, coming from upstairs, hit his conscience. His temper cooled. He allowed his mooma to seat him in the hammock.

'If you get charge fo murder, and you neck bruk, eh-eh, is me going lose. And what people going say? She could always get one next man, but when you neck bruk me could never get you back. You must not get hasty. But is good you put she in she place.'

Big-Bye's attention was riveted upstairs. Data's cries ached in him. He remained in the hammock thinking.

Night crept on the village but Big-Bye mooma's yard was quiet, unaffected by the Saturday evening bustle that went on outside.

As Big-Bye mooma penned the fowls in the backyard, she muttered to herself, 'Never in me born life me been go believe me own datin-law going give me hot-mouth. Is damn well right. This radio and newspaper and commercial eddication destroying young people. Chu chu chu. Them mouth only set to eat pork and beef. Gaad Shree Bhagawan... Is me fate. Me got to hold one jhandee...'

She exploded at the fowls who wouldn't go in the pen.

113

'And where is this man, eh?' she demanded. 'Where Big-Bye papa disappear?' It vexed her that despite all her efforts to curb his rum-drinking, he still escaped to the rum-shop as often as he could. Instead he study Gaad and do puja every Sunday morning is only rum he want.

And could be this same attitude which causing all this janjhat in this house, she pondered. She knew, too, that whenever a house was beset by domestic wranglings, however many prayers were said or religious works done, rarely did they help. The household never thrived. Sickness, losses, bad-luck and other calamities sucked the life from the house like a leech. But what about them top-top Hindu who eating souse and allowing them picknee to go cinema, and see English picture? she asked herself, locking the pen. Is people like them shoulda cover they face in the street. Eh-eh, but they face more bright than me and you. Tink this coulda happen in Estate?

Big-Bye took his dinner in a sullen mood. He didn't want to be disturbed by his mooma's presence. He worried over the incident, trying to decide in what respect he had been wrong in hitting Data. Her crying had stopped now and Big-Bye wanted to know if she had eaten dinner. He tried to weigh the incident, and concluded that he should have found out more about the cause of the story before hitting her. He could still see the fright in Data's eyes when he slapped her. He never wanted to hurt her. He loved her. The first woman he had loved. He had a compelling lust for her body.

'You wife get a sweet body. Better keep she in lock and key.'

'By, Big-Bye, when you lie down pon that puss you must be feel you in heaven...'

Big-Bye recalled his canecutting friends' teasing remarks. 'Only lucky man does get woman like she,' another friend had said. His chest had swollen with pride that midday, taking lunch under a mango tree in the canefields. Afterwards he felt that he could cut away a half-field of burnt sugarcanes on his own.

Got to find a way to ask Data pardon, he told himself, and hurried the rest of the meal, glad that his mooma was in the backyard.

'You done eat, beta?' his mooma asked affectionately when she came back in the house. She collected the wares and put them in the sink. She muttered to herself, saying murderation could have taken place, and where the hell was Big-Bye papa. 'Me waiting fo give he one dose. Wait til he come home,' she added sourly. 'Only fit to drink rum. Not even showing respect to me altar.'

Big-Bye felt sick. His stomach churned as though he had drunk polluted water from the canal. He didn't know what to tell Data. Guilt and fear mingled as he entered the upstairs cautiously. As he neared his bedroom, he called softly and hesitated: 'Data?'

No answer.

The door was ajar. He entered. Data sucked her tooth chu, and turned to the other side of the bed, dismissing Big-Bye. He advanced all the same and sat on the edge of the bed. 'You want me bring tea fo you?' he asked. He wanted to touch Data's thigh.

Chuuu... Data sucked her tooth again, ignoring him. Me going learn he one sense, she told herself, pretending to sleep.

Big-Bye touched her lightly.

Data squirmed as though stung by a marabunta. 'Na touch me,' she snapped in a low venomous tone, edging further away from him.

Big-Bye sighed helplessly: 'Me sorry, girl. Me wouldn't slap you next time.'

He edged towards Data, assuming a contrite attitude. 'Girl, me sorry. Tru tru,' he said, attempting to touch her again.

Data stiffened, locking her thighs, closing out Big-Bye's presence. I going punish you. You picking up to you mooma without knowing who is right and wrong. Tink me hungry fo man?

115

Big-Bye could find no way to placate Data. He tried to remember what experts like Bahadur said about how to woo a woman when she was angry. But no clue came to him. In helplessness he changed and slumped into bed, telling himself that if by tomorrow Data wouldn't speak to him, he would have to consult Bahadur.

Data pretended deep sleep.

It was much later in the night when Big-Bye papa reached home. He was drunk, mumbling old Hindi film songs. He staggered under the house, shouting for Big-Bye mooma.

'Is now you come, you drunken dog,' she barked in anger, accusing him of responsibility for all that had happened in the household.

'Chaach. You bring me food and shut you mouth,' he ordered, waving his right hand dismissively. He slumped in the hammock and hiccoughed as though he wanted to retch. Spasmodically he burst into old Hindi film songs, muttering names of old Hindi films he had seen.

'Is only this you good fo? Stuff rum day and night. Murderation nearly take place, and you nuh care one ass. You just out the house like jeptic.'

'Ah woman, shut you mouth!' he said wearily. 'Is you first jump pon doolahin.'

'What?' Big-Bye mooma snapped. She left the dinner on the eating table in the kitchen and waded under the house. 'You accusing me? You nuh get shame?' she added, pointing her fingers at him. 'Is this me punishment? Me come like everybody eye-pass. Is any piss-in-tail bady want push they finger in me face.'

'Bring me food woman. Ha ha ha. Is you mind get you so,' he mocked. 'Do more puja and you mind going come clean.'

'You shaitan devil,' Big-Bye mooma barked. He was treading on blasphemy. 'You cursing Shree Bhagawan nuh? If you drop down dead tomorrow, is who the cause, eh?'

'Ah woman, you going pray fo me?' His laughter echoed derisively, then he hiccoughed, rubbing his belly. 'I say, bring me food, woman,' he shouted and hiccoughed again.

Big-Bye mooma dashed in the kitchen, bursting in tears. 'Never know me ole age coulda be like this,' she lamented. 'Me gat to see pandit tomorrow tomorrow. Like is doolahin bring this kiss-me-ass janjhat. Me gat to see pandit.' Then impulsively she shouted: 'Aia Sumintra! Come see this eye-pass!'

Big-Bye could not sleep. He had heard everything. He knew he was wrong to hit Data, but he was afraid to wake her, and try to apologise to her for the third time.

On Sunday morning, Big-Bye mooma rose before day-clean, bathed, changed, and did puja. She was in a sullen mood. After doing puja she called on Sumintra, and both women headed for the temple. Sumintra did all the talking. It was a bright morning and other devotees streamed to the temple, walking on the dry muddam.

'You gat to put you foot on things, else is only cat-pat everyday,' Sumintra advised. She masked her real feelings. She felt Big-Bye mooma was trying to make herself a dictator in her household, using religion as the weapon. Many times her tongue had itched to tell her, 'This is different times. Young people should have their own say. Is no sin to dress in style, to eat what the tongue like. Eh-eh, after all food and clothes nah make fo dog and cat...' But Sumintra knew Big-Bye mooma's tongue and temper. Better let sleeping dogs lie, Sumintra had counselled, and kept her opinions to herself.

The temple was half-full; the devotees were mostly in their middle years with a smattering of older ones and a few young girls whose white ornhis made them stand out in the muted gathering. Most listened quietly to the pandit's rendering of the *Gita* in Hindi. The rapt attention of the most fervent and the aromas from the burning incense

117

sticks and freshly plucked flowers subdued even the most restive of the younger people. Every time the pandit paused and looked down at the gathering, a chorus echoed: 'Om shanti om.'

At the end of the ceremony, there was singing and the sharing of parsad. The pandit, middle-aged and fat, emerged from the decorated sanctum, garlanded clay gods on all four sides, and greeted favoured devotees. He was jovial, feeling quite pleased with the turn-out. At least the Hindu religion is still part of we lives, he told himself. But something gat to be done to win over the young people. Me nuh like how this modern education and fancy dress going. The birthday party. The christain preaching, eh-eh. The pandit felt a knot in his throat and his saliva turned sour. Got to do something, he urged himself, moving to greet another group.

Big-Bye mooma and Sumintra accosted the pandit, and led him to the temple verandah. They were old friends.

'Me nuh tink so, bahin,' the pandit whispered when he had listened carefully to everything Big-Bye mooma had said, including the notion that Data must have put 'trick' in Big-Bye's food so as to control him.

'You see bahin, you doolahin want be in the style, and when you object, janjhat take place,' the pandit explained.

'Is true panditji,' Sumintra joined. 'You gat to be very smart fo handle this generation. Young gal getting too much sense. They think they live in Town.'

'Is true,' the pandit replied, thinking about the growing number of brazen-faced young girls who dared look him in the face.

'One-one time youself must take out Big-Bye food, just to make sure. And must check he pillow to see if anything stuff inside,' the pandit advised.

'Yes, panditji,' Big-Bye mooma whispered conspiratorially, excited at the thought of what she might discover.

THIRTEEN

As soon as Big-Bye mooma arrived home from the temple she changed into house-clothes. The house was quiet, the tension of the day before less evident. Big-Bye, after failing to woo Data with sweet words, had given up and left the house to see Bahadur. Only Bahadur, who knew the ways of women, could advise him. Big-Bye papa was in the backyard working.

Throughout the day Data was in a sulky mood. She did the housework and the cooking, but hardly spoke. She was going to stop the advantage being taken of her, and as she prepared lunch, she debated the actions she would take. Is time enough to live me own life, she told herself, barely glancing at Big-Bye mooma who fretted by herself, trying to find things to do in the front yard.

After taking lunch, Data retired to her bedroom, still thinking over her strategy. Big-Bye mooma stayed in the hammock, baiting Data's movements. Since arriving home she had not had a chance to slip into Big-Bye's bedroom and examine his pillow, and to make an excuse to enter the bedroom would be too obvious. Besides, she had to examine both pillows and that would take time. She was not sure which of the pillows Big-Bye slept on. But she knew the day couldn't pass without her hunting for the 'trick'.

Big-Bye was defeated. He couldn't see Bahadur. His wife told him that Bahadur had gone with some folks to another village and wouldn't be back until nightfall. Big-Bye pouted his lips in frustration and left. None of his friends in the village was capable of advising him. Though many of them could boast of sexual encounters with prostitutes in Georgetown, Big-Bye doubted that this kind of experience could help him in his plight. Besides, he would feel awkward telling his friends about his situation. They would call him a little boy. 'You making de woman control you, eh,' they would mock. 'Is why you na give de woman one good fuck, eh. That is de only thing fo put she in place. Is not because you pissing fraff, you tink you is big man.'

He knew what they would say.

When he arrived back home he decided to try again with Data. He trod the stairs lightly, listening outside the bedroom door to see if he could tell whether she was awake. He was glad his mooma was sleeping and that his papa had probably gone out by the sea front. He had been talking about needing to cut brambles to support the sprangs of bora he was growing in the back yard.

He pushed open his bedroom door quietly, craning his head inside. Data was sleeping, her dress crumpled, exposing a part of her blue panty. Big-Bye felt an erection coming. At once he recalled how, when he was about fifteen, he and his friends used to haunt a particular shop bridge in the village. As soon as they spotted a girl or woman coming into the shop, they would jump down from the shop-railing, and pretend they were searching for aerated-bottle corks. They would go under the shop-bridge, still searching. As the woman or girl walked up the bridge to enter the shop, they would look up, peering through the cracks between the planks of the bridge. They would glimpse the female's panty, with their fingers already clutching their crotches. Later, if the day had not turned dark, they would seclude themselves among the trees growing by the railway line, betting which one of them could get the quickest erection. Then they would masturbate, focusing their imaginations on a particular panty and the mound it covered.

Big-Bye sat on the edge of the bed, his eyes still rivetted on Data's panty. Data didn't turn; she was breathing softly. Look like she sleeping, Big-Bye told himself. He got up and took off his pants and shirt. Then he quietly closed the bedroom door. He lay on the bed beside Data, wondering if he could arouse her without provoking her anger. He wanted her. His hardened penis pained him. He began caressing her thighs, playing with the string of her panty. Data didn't shift and her breathing was low. Shit, like this girl in deep sleep, he told himself. But I want she. I can't bear this thing. Then he recalled his canecutter friend, Sugrim. Sugrim was married. 'Sleep or na sleep. Once you want screw, take out the woman panty, play with she patacake, open she foot, and jump on she.' They had been drinking beers in Sarju's rumshop. The boys laughed. 'Is correct way. Eh-eh, if me get wife, and me want screw, you telling me I can't get. Schuuu. Passion or no passion, once I want screw I gat to get it...'

Big-Bye worked his fingers into Data's panty, caressing her pubic hair, straying his fingers further. His desire grew, and he knew that he would soon lose the power to hold back his orgasm. His fingers titillated her clitoris, but as he attempted to part Data's thighs and mount her, she woke up with a start and screamed. Big-Bye jumped off, his heart in panic.

'Is me, girl Data,' he said, frightened. His erection died. Desperately as he wanted her, he sensed that in some way he was taking something that was not his to take.

'Like you want choke me?' she accused, sitting sprawled on the bed. 'You is some beast that you must have my thing while me asleep? Or is you mooma and you plan kill me, na?'

'Is what-happening upstairs, doolahin? Like you seeing jumbie,' Big-Bye mooma shouted from under the house. Like she own obeah killing she. She believed the 'trick' in the pillow must have given Data a bad dream. As they had been coming back from the temple, Sumintra had mentioned that such 'tricks' could haunt the doer for two weeks after they had been placed inside a pillow. Is good. When you playing with fire, you bound to get burn, Big-Bye mooma thought with satisfaction.

'But but... me sorry me box you, girl. Is just me want do lil thing with you,' Big-Bye explained, his eyes beseeching her to understand. 'Me promise not to box you fo stupidness. Me mooma been wrong. Me know that.'

'Look Big-Bye, me nuh able with this thing. Is better me go away. Me nuh able live under you mooma petticoat,' Data said, testing him. Her strategy could only work if he did as she wanted. In order to gain her independence he must be persuaded to do her bidding.

'But, Data, me like you. We married, you know.' His tone was self-pitying. O Gaad, if she only left me, what me friends going say, he asked himself. Everyone agreed she was a good-looking girl: plump in bust, a curved waist, full hip, rounded face, coffee-coloured skin. When he was seen with Data in the streets Big-Bye was aware of the eyes admiring her. O Gaad, if she left me, is what people going say? They go say me one ignorant, blackskin, ugly boy. Data gave him status in the village. Were she to leave him, people would say she had found out what an ugly boy she had married. He would be the laughing stock, not his mooma. O Gaad, me nuh want that happen.

He reassured Data for the third time. He would never again hit her. And he would listen to her. Is time enough to think and act like a married man...

'Remember, don't eat back you word,' Data threatened, pointing her fingers. Then she got up off the bed.

'Never girl,' Big-Bye said firmly, holding her hands. Data made it clear she was in no mood for sex, but she told him that if *she* was in the mood, perhaps that night they might have a good time. Big-Bye nodded, emboldened, wishing now was night. He tried to raise Data's dress, but she slapped away his hands. 'Wait til night time, nuh,' she rebuked. Big-Bye saw that there was no getting around her and stretched for his pants and shirt. Me have to show this man he have to take some count of my liking, Data thought.

Big-Bye was the first to come downstairs. His mooma saw him in the kitchen. 'What happen beta? Like doolahin been trying to fight you?' she asked, getting out of the hammock.

'Nothing, Mai. Me and Data been gaffing, then me make one joke, and she halla out cause me pinch she,' Big-Bye lied, dishing out his food.

'Oh!' Big-Bye mooma sighed. 'But you must be careful,' she warned, tempted to ask him to examine the inside of the pillow he slept on. But suppose there was nothing there? Then Big-Bye would want to know why she asked. To make story short, meself going search them pillow, she promised. Can't make Data suspect anything. Come tomorrow... In the meantime she decided to play it smart. Talk sweet with Data who, she observed, was still sulky and uncommunicative. And if Data had stuck 'trick' in the pillow she might take it out if she think me acting suspicious. But I gat to know if she controlling me son. The pandit could be right. She returned to the hammock, and shouted across for Sumintra.

When Data came downstairs fifteen minutes later, Big-Bye was in the pit-latrine at the back. Big-Bye mooma entered the kitchen and said: 'Doolahin, you betta cook roti and dal, and make saltfish choka.' She spoke as affectionately as she could manage, but Data barely answered, gathering the wares to be washed. 'And you must fuget the quarrel. Which house nuh get teeth and tongue nowadays,' Big-Bye mooma added. Me gat to play it careful, so me could discover the trick, she told herself, and said, 'If you want me help you cook, tell me.'

'Arite,' Data replied. In order for Big-Bye to help her achieve her goal she had to play it careful. His mooma must know nothing of what she planned. She knew that any difference in views between herself and Big-Bye mooma could end in a quarrel and she didn't want to be deemed a warrish daughter-in-law. The assertion of her independence would have to be gradual and disciplined.

'But you mean to tell me this man nuh come home yet,' Big-Bye mooma said, trying to coax Data into conversation. She moved about under the house on the pretext of finding something useful to do. 'Suppose this man drop in by Moti and start drink rum? Me going tear he ass when he come,' she said to herself, but loudly enough for Data to hear. She wanted Data to know what a concerned mother-in-law she was, that she could not tolerate wrong things.

'Wait when he come,' she repeated as she entered the kitchen. She tried to make herself useful, to regain Data's trust and affection. Tomorrow, when she entered Big-Bye's bedroom, Data must not suspect anything. After all, is only one son me gat, and me nuh want none woman control he, she told herself. Who going look after me when me get ole and feeble? Who going do me dead-wuk when me dead? Can't trust this time young gal...

As soon as night fell, Big-Bye bathed and hurried into the bedroom, telling his mooma he was not feeling well. He had bolted through his evening meal, and gulped down the tea. Data lingered in the kitchen, washing the wares. Afterwards she set aside a little food in a small pot, and placed it on a shelf. This was done so that if good spirits visited during the night they would find food if they were hungry. Data did this every night before retiring. It had begun in her own household. 'You don't know who does visit you house in the night when you dead ah sleep,' her mother had said years ago when Data had asked her about this custom. 'They say devtas does visit people house in the night. Only people with good mind, and who doing puja every Sunday does get the visitation. Is no use you pray to them and you don't offer them something. When you seeing people prosper, mean they does leave food overnight fo them devtas. You hear?' Since then Data had regarded it as a sacred duty, and Big-Bye mooma had been pleased when she saw Data practising the custom the first week she was in the house. 'Good gal,' she had encouraged, 'meself does do it. But from now you going do it for we.'

When she had finished all the chores, Data asked Big-Bye mooma whether there was anything else she wanted.

'Na, you go sleep,' she told Data, and slumped in the hammock. She was waiting for Big-Bye papa to arrive. 'Is me and he when he come home. Since midday, eh,' she added. The night turned darker; crickets and beetles chirruped and croaked among trees and flowers.

After Big-Bye had fulfilled his sexual hunger, he lay beside Data on the bed, breathing quietly. One of his hands rested on her breast. He loved cupping her breast. 'We gat to start live ahwe own life, Big-Bye,' Data urged, and began mapping out some of her plans to him. She knew it would be tough at first, and they would face opposition from Big-Bye mooma, but they had to start asserting themselves at some point. She was not content to remain merely someone's daughter all her life. She was a married woman now; she had to think and act like one. Of course they would continue to cook in the same pot, share the same house; but decisions regarding *their* future would be made between herself and Big-Bye.

About nine o'clock the next morning Big-Bye mooma was idling under the house. Big-Bye and his papa had gone to the fields. Sun was up, and the morning took on a solemn look, the wind blowing quietly. She knew that Data took her morning bath at this time. Indeed, Data soon came downstairs with a towel wrapped under her armpits. Big-Bye mooma rushed upstairs and furtively entered Big-Bye's bedroom. She pounced on a pillow and began feeling it like someone probing a hen to see if it had an egg. Her ears listened for the slightest movement under the house. She knew Data always took a long time to bathe, yet she had to be careful. She rummaged the other pillow, her heart beating. She was puzzled. She couldn't feel anything like a knot. There was only a sponge. Tikkay she put the trick somewhere else, she wondered, roaming her eyes over the door-beam and window-sills, then searching them more closely. But she could find nothing like a knot. Can't believe it, she told herself, shaking her head. Suppose the pandit telling me one lie. Maybe Data put the trick one next place. But where... Then the fear of discovery struck at her bowels and she had to hurry out of the house for the latrine.

An hour later Sumintra joined her. Sumintra moaned as she sat on the bench near the hammock, lamenting the biting pains in her knee-joints. 'Is the backdam wuk,' she complained. 'Is bending you back whole day, and crossing water in canal. And wukkin in rain and sun. Gaad, backdam wuk in you bone...' She shook her head as if pitying herself. 'And is what me gat to show?'

Big-Bye mooma interrupted this monologue and asked: 'Sumintra gal, you know me na find no trick in them pillow.'

Sumintra got up, headed for the grass border, and spat out a mouthful of chewed black tobacco, acting as if in deep thought. She came and sat down again, sighing. 'Could be that doolahin na put none trick in pillow,' she said quietly. 'Could be doolahin is Big-Bye fus' woman. Could be doolahin love he. Na worry. We going watch doolahin behaviour. We going to know if she trick Big-Bye...'

Big-Bye mooma turned in the hammock, unconvinced. 'But me can't understand. Pandit say look in pillow.' She knew Data had Big-Bye under her spell. She would have to make discreet enquiries as to whether a 'trick' could be placed elsewhere than in a pillow. She tried to recall other methods women used to control their husbands.

For the next three days Big-Bye mooma couldn't reach any one in the village trusted enough to raise the question of the 'trick'. Lalo had been ill for a few days and it was not until Thursday midmorning that he was able to visit. She made sure Data had gone across to Chan, before raising the issue with Lalo. She had mixed feelings about Data seeing Chan, and though she was glad to see Data out of the house she warned her: 'Careful. Chan is a wise woman. And she eating beef.'

As Lalo told Big-Bye mooma all he knew about 'tricks', she noted how much older he was looking after his illness. The wrinkles on his body were more distinct, his skin looked dull and his hands shook as he drank water from the cup she offered him. 'Far as me know, bahin. If you clip head hair from man and write he name in white paper, then do same with woman, and you bury it in red cloth under one red flower plant, man never lef woman, if woman bury it.' Lalo lapsed into silence. After a while he shook his head. 'Only bad-minded woman do am such thing,' he mumbled. 'Proper Hindu woman don't do am such thing.'

Big-Bye mooma's turned to look at the flowers planted along the inner front paling. She barely listened to Lalo now. Her eyes examined each plant, dallying awhile on the ones which had red petals. She wanted to go and examine them straightaway, to see if any roots showed signs of disturbance, but she didn't want to create suspicion. She would examine the plants after the midday lunch when Data took her sleep.

The sun was at its hottest, the village drowsy, the only movements coming from the occasional woman walking the street to the market when, sweating heavily, Big-Bye mooma, using a short cutlass, dug-up all the flower plant roots which had red blossoms. She rummaged her fingers carefully between the dry cow manure and loosened earth moulded around the roots. After she had dug them all up and found nothing she cursed, hoping no one from the neighbouring houses had been watching. Can't trust people. She mopped her face, wishing the wind would blow more strongly to refresh her. Like Shree Bhagawan self against me, she whispered in self-pity as she moulded back the roots. But I gat to find this trick. Suddenly her bowels churned and she had to rush to the latrine. These sudden bowel-aches happened whenever she worried these days. It had never happened in the past. Is since doolahin start want get she own way. I gat to find this trick, control doolahin, and then me bowel control.

Data became more affable as the days passed. She had already planned her first move. Big-Bye mooma, too, masked her feelings. Her tone turned sweeter, and she volunteered to help Data whenever her workload seemed heavy. This way she was able to observe Data's behaviour keenly, though, so far, she had not been able to pick anything suspicious.

Big-Bye mooma vented her frustrations on her husband. She abused him as a drunkard, a wastrel, as a Hindu who failed to do his duty. Finally, early one night, Big-Bye papa exploded: 'Yes, you crocodile. You only know to swell up and quarrel like hatching fowl. Why you na ask Shree Bhagawan to clean you mind.'

Big-Bye mooma burst into tears. Then she turned hysterical, pretending a terrible headache. They were under the house. Big-Bye and Data were in the bedroom. Big-Bye knew his mooma was playing a trick on his papa, but wouldn't go down to make peace, though Data urged him to. 'Lef them. They going patch up just now,' he said.

But although it was still quite early, Big-Bye papa stalked upstairs to the big bedroom, slumped into bed, and pretended to sleep, snoring loudly. When she had closed the downstairs, Big-Bye mooma followed. Big-Bye papa snored even louder when she entered the bedroom. 'Musahar you,' she said in muffled tone, ears glued to Big-Bye's bedroom. Big-Bye papa stiffened his body.

128

The following Thursday night Big-Bye and Data made love. For Data, their love-making was still insipid, yet she cooperated until Big-Bye had satisfied his hunger. He was still hurried, unaware that he left her unsatisfied. But she recalled Chan's advice: 'Open you legs, and na get up when Big-Bye break in you. Allow the spence to go til in the womb.' Data did exactly that. She had thought she was pregnant, but the previous Tuesday morning she had started her menstrual course which lasted for five days. It had been delayed by two weeks. She had thick clots in the blood. Chan had said it was normal but urged her to get pregnant. 'You want people say you is barren? And you know them say barren people does bring badluck in house.'

When she did get up she wiped off a few drops of Big-Bye's juice with a rag, hoping she would become pregnant. Big-Bye mooma would feel happy. 'Me want hold me granchile before me dead,' she sometimes remarked, looking at Data openly. Data would bow her head, smiling.

In whispers Data told Big-Bye that she would try to get a stall in the market and begin selling provisions, greens and eggs. As soon as the stall began to show a profit, Big-Bye could rent a couple of acres of farm land aback Buxton village and begin farming. Also, he should begin to raise fowls and ducks to sell. 'We going build a big pen in the backyard, and we going to mind one-two turkey, girl,' Big-Bye agreed enthusiastically, glad at the thought of gaining his freedom from canecutting. His friends would say, 'Big-Bye, you is a betta man. Wukkin with youself. You shoulda praise your wife.' He could hear some of the remarks already.

Encouraged by his response, Data felt that it was time to be assertive. She rubbed Big-Bye's chest and said, 'Tomorrow is Friday. You getting pay afternoon time. You must give me you pay packet.'

'Arite,' Big-Bye said, hugging Data.

But when he was handed his brown pay-packet on

Friday afternoon at the small pay-office by the Lusignan roadside, Big-Bye began to realise the scale of Data's demand. He stood stock-still in a trance, in the middle of a noisy throng of sugar workers, some fixing up their drinking arrangements, others arguing because they believed they had been underpaid. Big-Bye stood alone. He put the pay-packet in his rightside pants' pocket, still in a daze. It was only when his friends urged him to come for their ritual weekly drink that he was provoked into action. 'Me na feel good, man,' he lied, clutching his head with one hand. He staggered awhile to make the act convincing, and moaned, 'Gaad, like I sick,' signalling that he wished to be left alone.

'You betta catch house, and nourish you back. Like you screwing the woman too much,' his friends said laughing, heading for the crowded rumshop across the public road.

Big-Bye's mind was in turmoil as he walked home past the makeshift market in the street in front of the pay office. How to hand Data his envelope, when for years, beginning with the first pay-packet, his mooma was accustomed to receiving it? As Big-Bye crossed the public road and headed into the dam that led to the village, the sweat gathered on his forehead and drained from his armpits. His head began to ache. But is how some boys who just get married giving them wife they envelope? And they say they used to give they mooma it. Is how they doing it? Big-Bye questioned, ignoring passers-by who hailed him. And suppose me give me mooma, Data going vex. And if me give Data is what me mooma going say? He recalled what Data had said: 'Is only when me start handle you money, then we going do what we plan.' And he had agreed.

Gaad help me, he begged, turning into the street that led to his house. The sweating grew even more profuse, as if he had contracted a sudden fever. He shivered. He didn't know what to do. He even lost his balance for a moment as he entered the yard heading for the kitchen. Data and his mooma were cooking; the smell of curried fish made him feel sick. He put down his working bag, sat on a chair and sighed. He felt dizzy. His right hand fidgeted in his rightside pants-pocket, his fingers playing with the pay-packet. His mooma watched him as she turned the rice boiling in the pot. The chula-fire was low. The dry redwood hardly smoked. His mooma walked up to him, and stretched out her right hand, palm open. She waited for the pay-packet. Big-Bye took it out.

'Big-Bye,' Data shouted, eyes domineering, hands akimbo.

Big-Bye hesitated, pay-packet in his right palm. His eyes vacillated between his mooma and Data.

Big-Bye mooma looked bewildered. She wanted to know what was going on. Why Big-Bye hesitated to give her the pay-packet. Impulsively she grabbed it out of Big-Bye's hand.

'Big-Bye,' Data shouted, her tone expressing the betrayal, contempt and anger she felt.

'Kiss-me-ass!' Big-Bye cried. He felt trapped, humiliated, his manhood threatened. Without thinking he dashed at Data, and let-go his right palm.

BLAI

Data staggered. His fingerprints showed on her left cheek. 'O Gaad!' Data screamed, and rushed upstairs. 'Me na want you. Me going away now now...' her tear-filled voice echoed as she entered the bedroom. Frantically she collected her clothes, dumped them into a grip, and headed downstairs.

Big-Bye mooma still couldn't understand what was going on. When Data reached downstairs Big-Bye mooma responded in the only way she knew. 'Doolahin,' she shouted, 'is where you going?'

Quickly Big-Bye got out of the chair he had slumped into. 'Data!' he shouted desperately.

'Me na want you! Me going away!' she cried as she walked out of the front gate.

Big-Bye felt as if he had been hit by a bullet. 'O Gaad,

Data! Na go away,' he pleaded, rushing behind her. 'Ow Data, na lef me!'

His mooma followed, shouting, 'Big-Bye. Let she go. Me going get nex woman fo you...'

'Me going with me wife,' Big-Bye shouted, following Data.

'O Gaad, Sumintra, come. Me doolahin did trick me son!' Big-Bye mooma called out, beating her chest in the street. 'Big-Bye, come back. Me gettin next woman to you...'

But Big-Bye had already turned into Market Street, still following Data, begging her to stop, oblivious of the folks watching them. He couldn't live without Data.

'Ow Shree Bhagawan, help me,' Big-Bye mooma pleaded, swaying her hands above her head. Then she turned into Sumintra's yard. 'Ow Sumintra. Me tell you that witch trick me son. Me tell you...'

FOURTEEN

'Don't touch me! Go touch you mooma!' Data snapped in a mixture of passion and insult when Big-Bye tried twice to grab her hands, pleading and beseeching as he followed her. 'Think me is one dog which you mooma want tie in chain? You picking fo she.'

'But Data, me beg you pardon,' Big-Bye implored quietly for the third time as they headed for the Public Road. He felt even more humiliated when he noticed that he was being observed scornfully by the youths who loitered by the roadside. He knew they would mock his subservience. 'Like he begging his wutliss wife not to leave he... Like he turn puppy-dog? He never see woman yet? Is man like them does make woman eye-pass we man. Make we turn Christmas blow-blow...'

Yes, Big-Bye knew what the talk would be in the rumshops, or when the boys were playing cards by the street-head. 'Chap, if you see how Big-Bye begging the woman just like beggarman begging at you door fo food.'

'Chu chu chu... man like them shouldn't get wife. True! they should put on one frock and walk the street. Rub powder on they face...'

'Boy! If was me, is cut-rass to play. Think any woman going to play they ass with me? Man done name man. God make them high. Is woman suppose to beg man, cause is man ruling the world, not woman...'

O Gaad! Big-Bye hated himself now, watching sideways

133

at the boys, quietly begging Data not to go away as she waited for a taxi. He tried to persuade her to talk and behave calmly, to act as though she was just going to spend the weekend at her mother's. Is what people going to say after they discover that Data left me, he asked himself.

He remembered the saying: 'Woman does only leave man when she know he acting like auntie-man.' Is me mooma caused it, he told himself, desperately hoping that Data would change her mind. If only me could act like a big man in front me mooma...

'Ow girl Data, me going to give you me pay packet next Friday. Me promise you on me knee.' And Big-Bye would have done it if it weren't for the boys who heckled and spat as though they were smelling dog-dung. One, unkempt and loosely dressed, said loudly: 'Woman like them does take man when they husband gone to work.'

Big-Bye heard, and knew the remark was meant for him. Is why me had to married, he asked himself, still pleading as Data got into a taxi.

She turned to face him. 'Don't follow me, Big-Bye,' she hissed with a force which took him by surprise.

He felt like an ants' nest crushed by a heavy footfall, like a mango left rotting on a tree. Data didn't want him and it was all due to his mooma's interference.

He cursed his mooma as he walked aimlessly in the village, feeling dazed, ignoring the boys as he walked past them. He didn't want to face his mooma. If me could only drop dead is better, he thought, feeling sick and worthless and defeated. Is why me can't act like a big married man? Is why me can't deal with woman. Is what really holding me back? His mind flashed to Bahadur. Is only he could tell me what to do now, he thought, heading straight for Bahadur's house.

Squashed in the taxi, Data began to feel that perhaps she had behaved childishly, but then reasoned that if she hadn't acted that way, Big-Bye would not have understood how serious she was, that she meant what she said about planning their future. She could only achieve those plans by first controlling their money, then getting Big-Bye mooma to see her way. She knew that a husband and wife should plan together, and she was certain, as night followed day, that once she could prove she was not barren, half her problems with her mother-in-law would be solved.

She had been thinking about all this for months. It had begun when she noted the relationship between Chan and Sumintra. At first she had thought that Chan was immensely daring, but then she had seen that Sumintra was tolerant and understanding, that she never tried to subject Chan to her ideas, and Chan never tried to impose hers on Sumintra. If only me and Big-Bye mooma could live like that, Data wished, recalling what Chan had once said to her: 'Look girl, if you na try to get you own way one-two time, Big-Bye mooma going to ride you like jackass. After all, you have you own mind. Think for youself. You is somebody. You is not Big-Bye mooma picknee.'

If me only could be like Chan, Data had wished. Chan get two children. Chan is a big woman. She word get weight. If only me could get pregnant quickly. Is then me could talk like Chan. Me won't have a curse to bear. Me going to be a full woman. Me make picknee, and Big-Bye mooma going to see with me. So she had thought.

Then Data smacked her tongue quietly, watching through the window as the taxi swung into the narrow redbrick road that led to her parents' house. Dusk had begun to gather, and they passed rumbling donkey carts laden with grass and firewood. It had become clearer to her that she wanted to be more than Chan, though she admired Chan's bold and independent spirit. No. Chan was just an ordinary housewife. She depending on she husband. In one way Chan still tie-down. The more Data thought about it, the more she resented the idea of being trapped in a position where 'you seeing the world like a blind goat'.

Not me. Oh no! Data wanted to be herself. Someone like the seamstress perhaps, in a position where she could do her own thinking, aspire to live her own dreams, start building a future for her unborn children. Her ideas about the provision business would be a beginning. Make things easier for Big-Bye. Yes! become herself. Her own person.

As the taxi braked in front of the Railway Line to allow a herd of rancid-smelling cattle to pass, it suddenly dawned upon Data how commonplace and insignificant her calling name was. Why had her mother insisted on calling her Data from the time she was a baby, not the name Savitri given to her by the pundit after he had consulted his Patra. Like me mooma always believe me going to be she lil daughter...

Me is not Data alone. Data. Everybody Data, she told herself, hating the name, thinking of the countless girls who answered to the name of Data. Me is Savitri. Her eyes brightened like a sudden crackling of flame in a fireheap. She saw herself as a distinct person, unique like the sun, a genip tree, a jamoon tree, wrapped in her own dreams, her own aspirations. If only people would call me Savitri now, she wished, impatient in the baking heat of the taxi, watching in irritation as the stubborn stragglers from the herd defecated and urinated idly by the side of the vehicle. The fat taxi driver blared the horn in annoyance, cringing his nose, and murdering the cattle with his eyes.

She knew Big-Bye would come for her. But now she would call the tune and he would have to dance to it until he realised he was a married man, and acted accordingly. Yes, this Big-Bye must able to tell his mooma what he thought, what their plans were. Must able to be his ownself at all times, sturdy like a cork tree withstanding the wind's daily assaults.

Deep down Data knew that Big-Bye needed her, but she vowed not to take undue advantage of this need; she would use Big-Bye against his mooma only when the situation warranted. But first, Big-Bye had to see his own position, then he might begin to act like a full-grown man towards his mooma.

As the taxi approached her house she made two resolutions. She would be going back with Big-Bye only on condition that he swore to give her his pay-packet. That would be a start in her struggle. She would then be in a position to know how the household was being managed; she would learn the real value of money. What had to be spent. How much to save. How to use their money wisely in furthering her dreams. At the same time she would encourage Big-Bye to venture into the rearing of fowls and ducks, some of which could be sold, and the money saved for initial investment in the business. For the time being she was prepared to endure Big-Bye mooma's tantrums, as long as Big-Bye was really on her side.

She knew too that in due course she would have a child, and then she would be treated with more respect by Big-Bye mooma and her views taken more seriously. She would have proven herself a woman.

But, even after she had led him to see her way, could she rely on Big-Bye to stand up to his mooma whenever she tried to subject them both to her authority? She would have to hope so.

The other resolution centred around the word doolahin. She had come to hate the word even more than the name 'Data'. It sounded so bashful, like a bird penned in a cage, or a bride veiled in an ornhi while speaking to her father-in-law. She didn't want to be addressed as doolahin any longer. She didn't want to be treated as a protected bride, fed, pampered and chided whenever Big-Bye mooma or the neighbours felt like it. Oh no! She saw herself like Chan in this respect: courageous and independent-minded. She would continue to show Big-Bye mooma the respect due to her as her mother-in-law, but she would tell Big-Bye to tell his mooma not to address her as doolahin any longer. He would have to be persuasive and stern, perhaps saying, 'Mai, you know Data is not a doolahin now. And me does feel bad when you call she doolahin...' What she really wished though was that they would call her Savitri now instead of Data. Think me is everybody daughter? But how could she tell them that?

By the time the taxi braked in front of her house she had already made up her mind how she would live her life. She would have to deal with the conflicts that were bound to brew until Big-Bye mooma understood that different ways had to be accepted.

'Girl, this is modern time. Mankind going to the moon. Is not Estate time where the driver leading you like mule.' This was the kind of talk Data liked to hear.

Perhaps she could enlist Sumintra; let her coax Big-Bye mooma to understand that she should be addressed as Savitri not doolahin, or Data.

She knew Big-Bye would be coming for her, and she would ask him to stay awhile, spend the night perhaps. His mooma wouldn't like that, but Data felt she had a reason in doing so. Let he mooma do some thinking during we absence. Let she examine she self, and see how she acting like a mother hen.

'You is just Big-Bye fo namesake,' Bahadur said after listening to Big-Bye's plight. 'Think me mooma could tell me how to live me life? And think me taking eye-pass from wife, eh?' Bahadur smacked his tongue pityingly, as he sat in a vest and a worn-out short pants knitting his cast-net under the house. His wife, Suruj, affecting a kind of assured tranquillity, tended the garden. Big-Bye thought she looked content among the plants. If it were only Data.

'But man Bahadur, like me can't go against me mooma,' Big-Bye said helplessly, sitting on the bench, watching Bahadur who seemed to have an easy mastery of everything, fingers moving deftly with the cotton twine. Bahadur look like he ain't get one thing to study; as if he is he own big man, Big-Bye thought.

'You ever notice one fowl hen and them chicks?' Bahadur added, turning to Big-Bye. 'When the chicks small they running behind the fowl, but soon as them chicks tun fowl, is different. Sometime the fowl not even know she own chicks. Is just so with people. Only thing is that people know where they come from, and know they parents. But them chicks, when they tun fowl, have to fend fo theyself. Is just so with people. How long you could live under you mooma skirt? Man Big-Bye, you making me hand fall. You done mount woman, and you still acting like one flower tree which bending when wind blow...'

Bahadur shook his head, as if he was annoyed with Big-Bye; then he retrieved a cigarette from on top of his right ear, tapped one end gently on his left thumb, smacking his tongue, before lighting it. He inhaled, exhaled, paused, watching Suruj as she bent among the plants in the back garden.

Like this Bahadur master everything, Big-Bye told himself, feeling both slightly affronted and wishing he had Bahadur's commonsense. This Bahadur acting so certain, know how to live life, sure of himself like one coconut tree which know it going to bear coconut. Shit!

And Big-Bye knew Bahadur didn't mince matters, never allowed himself to slave to any woman. He recalled what Bahadur told him once: 'The day you make one woman ride you, you finish like cigarette. Always be the man but listen to the woman cause a woman could teach man sense. You see, a woman does see things with a different eye. Me always tell you that. But the moment you make one woman tie you by you neck like you mooma, chu chu chu, you could never be you self. Be you own man. Woman does respect man only when man be they own self. Boy, Big-Bye, like cockroach take away you commonsense...'

As Bahadur returned to his cast-net, Big-Bye's thoughts

seemed jumbled like burnt sugarcanes coiling and tumbling into each other in the fields. He wrestled with his thoughts, trying to define a position, an approach from which he could take action. Is why me can't handle meself between me mooma and Data sameways me handling me cutlass with them canes? True! Bahadur approaching things like a big man. More than ever Bahadur's remarks made sense to Big-Bye: 'Think me want kill meself in canefield where them driver tie you neck with rope. Eh-eh! that is not fo me. Me damn independent catching fish. And in the meantime me still thinking what to do to have more independence. Ha boy! You have to be you ownself, not somebody else. Is the only way people going to respect you.'

Big-Bye felt a heatedness in his body. This was what Data was trying to tell him. Bahadur was right. You should listen to the woman cause a woman could teach man sense. After some time he got up, pacing under the house, recalling Data's words: 'Is only when me handling you money, we could able to plan we future.'

The woman know what she doing. Ideas coming from she inside like Bahadur. God! If me coulda only see eye-to-eye with she, things woulda never turn out in this way. Me been blind, he lamented, seeing that all this while he had been tied to his mooma like a baby still suckling. Data been seeing through everything; she had said to him one night: 'Big-Bye, is how long you going to live under you mooma?'

He had been too wrapped up with her body to realise what sense she made. As he sat on the bench he felt ashamed of himself, chastened in comparison to Data's intelligence. He began to see her not only as a woman whose body he lusted for, whom he had begun to fall in love with, but a person possessed of a deep commonsense, like Bahadur who acted so sure and free like a bird in the sky. With her guidance he would be able to break away from his mooma's grasp. Yes! Data could advise him how to act, lead him along the road to discover himself. Become a real man like Bahadur.

He smiled to himself like a hungry child catching sight of food, unfettered by his mooma's sharp eyes. He felt roused from a deep, hypnotic sleep.

Bahadur said drily, mockingly: 'Big-Bye, you acting like a real shirt-tail boy. People should call you lil-boy, not Big-Bye.'

He felt a stab in his groin as if someone was assaulting his manhood. He flushed with offence, but had to conclude that Bahadur was damn-well right. He shuffled uncomfortably on the bench. Me is Big-Bye for namesake. Is like a mockery.

And as he grasped the irony of his name, he began to see too the true essence which it embodied. He recalled Deo who had been given the nickname 'the Big-man' because he acted more advanced than his fourteen years, a force-ripe boy putting on what he thought were mature attitudes. That is how Data sees me, he acknowledged.

And when Bahadur turned to him and said, 'You better go back fo you wife. Data is a good woman, and she look wise,' he had already seen in Data not only the body he craved but a source of his own growth, loving companion and guide rolled into one. Yes! this was the first time he had seen himself as he truly was. She would be his mirror, honest, critical. It would be hard, but it was the only way he could find of dealing with his mooma. She would have to learn to treat him like a married man, able to think for himself. If she didn't do that they were bound to clash. But first, perhaps, he had to behave like a married man.

Bahadur stopped his knitting, turned once again, and faced him, stroking his stubbled face: 'Don't try to vex you mooma. See with she. But let she see eye-to-eye with you, too. Is you wife have to make you a man, not you mooma. Is a wife does make a man a full man.' Then Bahadur dismissed the topic and resumed his knitting.

141

But Big-Bye felt he had already understood. Now, he was restless to go, feeling he had suddenly matured ten years, silently thanking Data and Bahadur for it. Me is a man, he muttered to himself, telling Bahadur he was going for Data.

As soon as Big-Bye mooma saw her son enter the yard, she was sure she had won a victory, that no matter how adverse or bitter the circumstances, Big-Bye would not neglect her, or 'turn his back on his own mooma who bring him in the world,' as the saying went.

But Big-Bye barely acknowledged her presence as he went upstairs, and she was too wrapped up in self-congratulation to perceive Big-Bye's cool attitude towards her. She was excited, pacing in the kitchen, 'Doolahin tink she is the only woman in the world. She want control you. She never make picknee? She know one mooma feelings? Me know she trick you, but the trick not working. And me na want she put back she foot in me house. Tink she body get gold and diamond? Have to tell Sumintra everything...'

Big-Bye mooma set the kitchen in order, planning how she would adjust herself once again to running the household as it had been before Big-Bye married. Me foot still strong, she whispered, though she was already scrutinising a few young girls in the village who looked like good, quiet Hindus, one among whom could become Big-Bye's next wife. Yes! she sighed as though she had already seen the chosen girl. She have to be straight like a coconut tree, and no skin-teeth and laugh, laugh, she told herself, wishing Data were dead. 'Want take away me son? Dry he back?'

Big-Bye, dressed in his visiting clothes, came downstairs and informed his mooma lightly that he was going out.

'Don't stay out late, son. And wipe doolahin out you mind,' she said, believing deeply that he would always be her own property.

Big-Bye looked at his mooma intently. He saw how

142

domineering and insensitive she was, but also how small and shrivelled. He felt anger, pity and love and cursed himself for his confusion. He would continue to show her due respect, give her his ears but with a reserved judgement now. He walked briskly out of the yard, a puzzling sadness welling under his resolution, his urgency to reach Data and sort out matters with her. His mooma called out after him but he did not look back.

As he headed for Data's village, he felt renewed. He would have to find a way of dealing with the boys who had leered at him earlier by the Public Road. Yes! They would mock him, but he told himself it was they who were small, hiding their weakness and uncertainty under the big-man's talk.

As he followed a narrow street to the Public Road, his eyes were struck by a tall coconut tree in one of the neighbouring yards. It bent and swayed in the stiff Atlantic breeze, but each year grew surely, tall and defiant, towards the sun. He quickened his footsteps for Data's village.

ABOUT THE AUTHOR

Rooplall Monar was born in a mud floor logie on the Lusignan sugar estate, East Coast Demerara, in 1945. His parents were both caneworkers. The family moved to Annandale Village in 1953 to a houselot with its own plot. This, much extended over the years, remains Monar's home. He attended Lusignan Government school, Buxton Congregational School, Hindu College and Annandale Evening College. He has worked as a teacher, accounts clerk, freelance journalist, broadcaster and practitioner of folk healing (herbal cures). In 1987 he was awarded a special Judges' Prize for his contribution to Guyanese writing.

ALSO BY ROOPLALL MONAR

BACKDAM PEOPLE ISBN 0-948833-00-9, 1985, £5.99
A landmark in Caribbean writing, these stories, written in the Hindi-influenced Creole of the people, evoke the inner world of the Indo-Guyanese sugar estate workers between the 1930s and the early 1950s when the estate communities broke up.

Frank Birbalsingh writes: 'The success of Monar's comic treatment is that it enables him to present scenes of gross violence and brutality without sentimentality. We laugh... but do not ignore the cruelty, pain and suffering involved...'

KOKER   ISBN 0-948833-05-X, 1987, £5.99
In this his first poetry collection, Monar looks for authentic roots in the limbo between decayed ancestral tradition and the oppressive history of cane labour. It is only in the hesitant native tradition of a creolised Indo-Guyanese culture that Monar sees sources of growth. *Koker* won a special award in the 1987 Guyana Literary Prize.

HIGH HOUSE AND RADIO ISBN 0-948833-12-2, 1994, £6.99
These stories explore the stresses of a sugar estate community's transition from communalism to the individualism of village life in a period of great turbulence in Guyana. Trickster strategies and a desperate search for meaning find equal voice.

Visit the Peepal Tree website and buy books online at:
www.peepaltreepress.com